SOFT DUTY

By
Michael R. Ellis

"Cold War Intrigue"

Senior Chief Rigney Page needs time to recover physically and emotionally from a decade of counterespionage missions. He requests a soft duty assignment stateside. ONI accommodates his request.

But fate provides no rest for the courageous. Soon after reporting to his stateside soft duty assignment, Rig is contacted by *The Guardians*; and they ask for his assistance.

Rigney Page Adventures

UNCONQUERABLE

(INVICTUS)

By William Ernest Henley

Out of the night that covers me,
Black as the Pit from pole to pole,
I thank whatever gods may be
For my unconquerable soul.

In the fell clutch of circumstance
I have not winced nor cried aloud.
Under the bludgeonings of chance
My head is bloody, but unbowed.

Beyond this place of wrath and tears
Looms but the Horror of the shade,
And yet the menace of the years
Finds, and shall find, me unafraid.

It matters not how strait the gate,
How charged with punishments the scroll,
I am the master of my fate:
I am the captain of my soul.

1980

1

Task Force 152 Field Office
USNAVSUPPACT Naples, Italy

Senior Chief Rigney Page sits in the office of his current mission controller, Commander Mallory. Both are tall, rugged looking men in their thirties, Mallory being older by six years. Both descend from Northern European ancestry as exhibited by Rig's reddish-brown hair and reddish complexion and Mallory's sandy colored hair and pale complexion. Both are trim and fit and present a commanding image when in uniform. However, on this Sunday morning, they are both in Italian style civilian clothes.

"I finished your report on Bella Heinzler's defection," Mallory advises. "Good job on getting her to the safe house."

"It became easy after she understood that her commie bosses were out to kill her."

"Your report claims she thought she was shooting burglars when she killed her associates in that beach house. Do you really believe that?"

"Yes," Rig affirms. "She was totally shocked when we removed their ski masks and she recognized them."

Mallory advises, "The Carabinieri reports that no bodies were found in that Barletta beach house, but the Carabinieri forensic team did find pools of blood. Their investigation led them to the house's owner, *Turismo Internazionale*, who claims the house was last reserved by one of their employees, Bella Heinzler, who has disappeared without a trace. Her bank accounts have not been touched and her apartment still has her personal belongings. The kennel where she placed her cat before departing for Barletta states that she planned on picking up her cat on the following Monday."

Rig nods his head and expresses understanding as he concludes, "The evidence indicates she is a victim of foul play—murdered maybe—kidnapped maybe."

"Yes," Mallory agrees, "and the U.S. Government has no plan to inform the Italians otherwise."

Rig questions, "I assume her pistol will never see sunlight again, right?"

"That's my understanding," Mallory

confirms. "Hidden deep in some safe in a CIA underground storage facility."

Rig express thoughtfulness as he stares out the window of the third-floor office. He appraises the view of the Agnano basin. He has read the history of Agnano and knows it is part of the Campi Flegrei Region of Naples—an ancient volcano crater, popular among both ancient Greeks and Romans for its famed hot sulfurous springs.

"I really enjoy Europe," Rig says in an affectionate tone. "Sometimes, I think I enjoy it more than Southern California." Rig's teenage years surfing the beaches of Southern California flash through his mind.

"Are you changing the subject?" Mallory asks.

"Might be," Rig expresses in a resigned tone. "This is the timeframe at the end of my missions when I am told that I will be transferred soon."

Mallory explains, "Eventually, the Carabinieri's investigation will lead them to you as Bella Heinzler's boyfriend. They will want to question you. ONI and CIA do not want you available for that. You are being transferred stateside before Italian authorities can issue a

Stay in Country Order."

Rig nods and expresses acceptance; then asks, "When?"

"Next week," Mallory answers. "We are working a deal with COMSUBGRU EIGHT to release you without a replacement."

"Ya know, I have never completed a full tour of duty anywhere."

Commander Mallory attempts to assess Rig's disposition; he asks, "Are you becoming weary of counterespionage missions?"

Rig casts a quizzical stare at Mallory that expresses: *where did that come from?*

"Rig, you have been working counterespionage undercover missions for thirteen years. The stress can take a toll on you. Such stress is common among operatives such as yourself."

"Quitting is not on my mind," Rig states in a slightly defiant tone. "My life is too exciting to quit, and I feel like I am contributing significantly to defeating evil.

"I became emotionally involved with Bella before she became a counterespionage target. I blame the incompetence and arrogance of your predecessor for that.

"Bella Heinzler is a good, decent person

who was brainwashed early in life. Evil almost destroyed her. She saved herself and me by turning her training on the evil that trained her.

"The Communist Alliance has tentacles that reach into all aspects of European life, both lawful and unlawful. I worry for her safety because I fear that the CIA relocation program cannot hide her from the evil that searches for her. I worry about it so much that I cannot focus on the details of my duties."

"Maybe you just need a long vacation," Mallory suggests.

Rig does not respond to that. He asks, "Do you know what I will be doing stateside?"

"I was told to cut orders for Task Force 152 DET Cheltenham, Maryland. That means you will be assigned to headquarters. I don't know how long you'll be there."

"Not surprised," Rig responds. "I am due for the full range of physical fitness tests and psychological tests."

Commander Mallory expresses a confident smile as he says, "Senior Chief, you won't have any problem with those tests."

Rig states in a doubtful tone, "Once I felt unconquerable. Now, I am not sure."

2

The Trajan Consortium
Switzerland

Le Haut Château sits on the side of a hill overlooking Lake Geneva. The five-century-old, stone-faced Renaissance structure stands three stories high, includes ten-bedrooms, and is located inside a compound with several small utility buildings. The compound is enclosed by a five-foot-thick, twelve-foot-high stone wall.

The wall contains modern alarms and video security systems. The single gate has one uniformed armed-guard stationed at all times and two uniformed armed-guards continuously walk the wall.

The security center is located on the château's first floor in the north corner. Security cameras with audio listening devices surveil all rooms and halls except for bedrooms and bathrooms.

Forty-eight full-time employees comprise the château's security, servant, and management staff. The staff is permanently in place at the château.

The seven directors of *The Trajan Consortium* sit at a horseshoe shaped conference table in the château's library. The six-thousand-book library is the largest room in the château and contains a number of rare books valued in six figures.

Werner Braune is a cofounder of *The Trajan Consortium* and he is the current chairman of the board of directors. The origin of *The Trajan Consortium* dates back to 1946 when Werner was in his second year at the University of Oxford. Braune and several classmates formed a workgroup as part of a class project to develop solutions for recovering Europe from the ravages of World War II. They originally named their workgroup *The Trajans,* after the Roman Emperor Trajan who unified the elements of power in the Roman Empire and who earned the loyalty of all Romans through honest, effective, and benevolent government.

Werner and other members of *The Trajans* were close to the problems in post WWII Europe because their fathers owned international businesses that were involved in rebuilding Europe. Their fathers complained about each country's snail-paced and incompetent bureaucratic government. International businesses that sold goods for Europe's reconstruction had to adapt to each country's unique regulations and purchasing processes. American reconstruction money added more frustrating bureaucracy to the process.

Werner and his classmates in *The Trajans* workgroup descended from that elite class of non-royalty Europeans who became wealthy during the early years of the Industrial Revolution. The fathers of *The Trajan* members inherited their business like their fathers did before them.

During the twenty years between World War I and World War II, Werner's father—like the fathers of his Trajan classmates, rebuilt their international businesses. So, when World War II ended, those businessmen already knew how to quickly reestablish their supply chains and customer bases. As was the case after World War I, their primary customers were governments of war-torn countries. And, as was the case after World War I, government bureaucracy was the major obstacle to World

War II reconstruction progress.

The Trajans believed that the solution to Europe's post war problems was to form a single European government to smooth post-war rebuilding. Eventually, those rich elitist businessmen who were the fathers of *The Trajans* became the significant forces behind the establishment of the European Common Market.

The Trajans continued their association after graduation. Back then, continuing *The Trajans* was justification for yearly reunions. During those reunions, they expanded their discussions on how to form a single European government with themselves as the governing directors.

In their arrogance, they renamed their group *The Trajan Consortium*. They allowed membership to other young and rich European businessmen who also believed in the establishment of a single European government ruled by their consortium. *The Trajans* eventually inherited their fathers' businesses, providing them with power to establish substance to their plans to rule Europe.

The Trajan Consortium remains a secret

society whose existence is known only to its member. Their secrecy is essential to their objective of establishing a single European government under their control. Secrecy is essential because their methods are sometimes illegal and treasonous, including acts of espionage or sabotage when necessary.

On several occasions, outsiders came close to uncovering the consortium. Those outsiders became victims of deadly accidents.

Currently, *The Trajan Consortium* membership includes 39 international businessmen whose citizenship includes most of Western Europe. The businesses of members employ millions of people worldwide. Their combined net worth totals $1.6 trillion. They control 35 percent of the worlds transportation services.

The total membership meets once each year. The purpose of the yearly meeting is to develop actions that improve and expand their business and actions that move them closer to ruling Europe under a single government.

The board of directors meet quarterly to measure progress. Minor adjustments to process are made at the discretion of the board. Major adjustments are voted on by the total membership at yearly meetings.

Today, the directors are constructing a strategy to prevent Ronald Reagan from winning the U.S. Presidency away from the current first-term president, Jimmy Carter. *The Trajans* fear that Reagan will go to war with Iran over the American hostages situation—an action that President Carter has refused to do. *The Trajans* also fear Reagan's campaign promise to increase U.S. domestic oil production. Reagan's actions will reduce the flow of oil from the Middle East, which will cost members of the consortium billions of dollars in oil transportation revenue.

The directors believe that as long as Jimmy Carter is president, he will keep the American hostages situation in the current stalemate and will not allow an increase in U.S. oil production. The directors believe firmly that the status quo will keep their oil transportation revenues increasing at a steady rate.

The vice-chairman turns toward Werner Braune and asks, "The United States is in your area; what have you done to prevent Ronald

Reagan from being elected?"

Werner Braune responds, "We are funding a number of Political Action Committees that publish propaganda against Reagan, and I have established an underground operation to sabotage the Reagan campaign. I have recruited four, radical, Marxist operatives who specialize in political sabotage. Each operative is assigned a geographic area: Eastern United States, North Central United States, South Central United States, and Western United States. Each of them already had his own organization in place when I recruited them. The additional funding I have provided has allowed them to expand operations."

"Radical Marxists?" the vice-chair questions. "Don't they know who you are?"

"Yes," Braune affirms, "but currently we have the same objective, preventing Ronald Reagan from becoming president. We are in agreement with those Marxists that we want Jimmy Carter to serve a second term. These Marxists have been working on that for a year. They were enthusiastic to team with me because of my influence and my funding to expand their operations."

One of the directors asks, "If they are

13

Marxists, why do they want to keep Jimmy Carter in power? America has its own socialist and communist political parties."

"Yes, America has socialist and communist parties," Braune affirms. "However, those parties have no power. These Marxists view Jimmy Carter as the lesser of the two evils. According to these American Marxists, their chances of pushing through redistribution of wealth programs are easier with Carter in power than with Reagan in power. According to them, Reagan is a budget hawk who campaigns to reduce taxes and reduce government spending.

"These Marxists operatives of mine tell me that their numbers are increasing in news organization, education, judicial system, and government. They believe that by the middle of the next century their numbers will be strong enough to control the outcome of America's elections. Until then, they publish anti-America, anti-capitalism propaganda and chisel away at America's capitalist economy."

A director predicts, "A socialist America would be a financial boost to our consortium."

All the directors nod agreement.

3

Task Force 152 Support Office
Cheltenham, Maryland

The two-story red-brick building that houses the ONI Support Office stands against the wooded area on the west side of the small U.S. Navy installation. The ONI building stands unidentified except for the building number. Those navy personnel assigned to other command units on the base refer to the building as the *spook building*, knowing only that navy spies work there.

Room 4 inside the *spook building* serves as a general purpose office and is not assigned to anyone in particular. Navy gray is the common color of the furniture and walls.

Commander Sally Macfurson sits at the only desk in the room. Senior Chief Rigney "Rig" Page sits in a comfortable armchair in a corner. In compliance with the Plan of the Day, they both wear Service Khaki uniform.

Sally and Rig first met thirteen years ago

when she worked as a civilian librarian at the Naval Submarine Base in Groton, Connecticut. He was a third class petty officer attending Submarine Radioman Schools on the same base.

Rig was immediately attracted to the petite, sexy redhead with bright green eyes. She was immediately attracted to the tall and ruggedly handsome sailor with a quick wit and inquisitive mind. They were intimate and spent many nights together.

Rig was bewildered by her attraction to him because he was convinced he was not in her league. Sally was fluent in several European languages. She had earned her Master's Degree in European History from a prestigious New England university and was working on her PhD. Sally came from a wealthy New England family. Rig came from a working class background in Southern California.

Three months after they first met, Rig was recruited to work undercover for the Office of Naval Intelligence, and he was transferred from Groton. At the time of his transfer, Sally was unaware of his recruitment by naval intelligence. She was saddened by his departure and interpreted his transfer as navy routine.

Sally became unwittingly involved in Rig's first mission and was placed in a life-threatening situation. The reality of the evil in the world motivated her to transfer from a life in academia to a life working in naval intelligence. Over the years, Sally was Rig's controller for several missions.

Their romance continued after Sally became a navy officer working in naval intelligence. Rig often thought that he and Sally would marry someday, after he discharged from the navy and no longer engaged in dangerous missions.

Then, during his last mission, he met and fell in love with Bella Heinzler, an alluring Italian beauty whom he helped defect from the life of a communist operative. That mission drained him physically and emotionally. Now, Rig is no longer certain about his future. He constantly aches to see Bella again.

Doctor Williamson, the ONI psychiatrist, prescribed a week's vacation in the warm sunshine. Then, Admiral Watson ordered Rig on vacation. Rig chose the Bahamas.

"How was your scuba vacation in the

Bahamas?" Sally asks.

"Excellent scuba diving," Rig answers. "Also did some deep sea fishing. It was a relaxing week."

"Were you alone?" Sally inquires in a not so hidden tone of jealous speculation that he was not alone.

She knows something changed Rig's manner during his Naples mission. He has become distant and he often appears preoccupied with thoughts. In the past when Rig returned to D.C., he was attentive and romantic toward her but not so much this time.

Sally is in love with Rig and has been since their days in Connecticut thirteen years ago. Several years ago, she became aggressive and told Rig she wanted to marry him. Rig said no because his occupation is dangerous and could place her in danger again. And one of them would need to leave the navy. Rig's reasoning was logical, and Sally accepted it.

Rig expresses a caring and thoughtful smile toward the woman with whom he has had a long and loving relationship. She is six years older than him, but you would not know it by looking at her. At the age of thirty-nine, Sally is still a beauty. She still has that dark auburn hair, much shorter now because of navy grooming regulations. Her petite body is still perfectly shaped, thanks to a rigid diet and daily exercise. Her face is still as lovely as the first time he saw her. Until he met Bella, Sally was the most important woman in his life.

Bella entered the CIA's Protection Program. Rig has no idea where she is and is concerned that he will never see her again.

"I was alone last week," Rig replies while looking in to her eyes and expressing sincerity and honesty.

Sally believes him because he has no reason to lie. They have a noncommittal relationship and they both have had intimate relationships with others and they have been honest with each other about it.

His romances with other women, including Bella, have not diminished his feelings for Sally Macfurson.

Whenever she sees Rig, she is stunned by his rugged good looks. He is a masculine, handsome man who stands just over six-feet and has the body of an Olympic swimmer. His reddish-brown hair and piercing green eyes tell of his Viking heritage.

When Rig comes to D.C., she clears her

19

social calendar. In the past when Rig was in D.C., they spent most of their off time together. This time, it's different. When he returned from Italy six weeks ago. His lack of interest in work and constant preoccupation with distant thoughts was obvious to her and to his superiors.

"Would you like to have dinner in my apartment tonight?" Sally asks, unable to hide her anxious anticipation. "I have the latest James Bond movie on video tape. We can watch it after dinner."

"Yes, I would like that very much," he answers with sincerity and interest. "May I bring my overnight bag?"

"Of course," Sally responds happily, hoping their relationship is returning to normal.

Sally shuffles some papers on the desktop, indicating they are about to get down to business.

Rig anxiously waits to learn what comes next in his naval intelligence career as a counterintelligence operative.

"I have some questions for you to answer before we discuss your next assignment. Since returning from Italy, you appeared distracted, distant. Is there something on your mind that you want to share with naval intelligence?"

Rig understands that Commander Macfurson asked an official question and not a personal one.

"I covered that with the shrink before I went on vacation. I will leave it up to him to reveal what he thinks necessary."

Sally states, "I have a few questions on a different matter?"

"Questions for the record?" Rig asks.

"Yes, for the record," Sally affirms. "These questions come from the Naval Investigative Service. They read your ONI debriefing transcript, hoping to gain facts regarding two investigations they are conducting."

Rig expresses curiosity and says, "Okay. Go."

"Depending on your answers, you may be required to give a deposition under oath and or testify under oath at courts-martial."

"Wouldn't that risk my cover?" Rig asks; his eyebrows are arched.

Sally responds, "NIS tells me the subject courts-martial, if they occur, will be behind closed doors and classified. ONI will ensure your cover is maintained."

"Okay. Go," Rig responds.

"I am recording this to be later transcribed to typed copies. The recording will be demagnetized after transcription and the typed copies will be sent to NIS." Sally turns on the desktop tape recorder.

"This recording is classified top secret. This is a recording of Commander Macfurson conducting a classified interview with Senior Chief Rigney Page. Commander Macfurson and Senior Chief Page are the only persons present. Copies of this interview will have restricted distribution: One copy to the ONI *Operation Defender* file and one copy to Naval Investigative Service."

Sally thumbs through some papers on the desk. She finds the NIS questions.

"What was your association with Italian national Bella Heinzler?"

"She was the target of my last mission—part of *Operation Defender*."

"What was the objective of your mission?"

"I was directed to turn her against the communist organization she worked for and convince her to defect to the United States."

"Were you successful?"

"Yes."

"Did you and Bella Heinzler ever discuss a

U.S. Navy officer named Robert Sweeney?"

"Yes."

"When did this discussion occur and what did Bella Heinzler tell you about Robert Sweeney?"

Rig interrupts the interview. "Commander, please turn off the recorder."

Sally turns off the recorder.

"Sally, all of Bella's U.S. military contacts were discussed with the CIA interrogators during those ten days in Italy just prior to her being taken into the CIA defector program. You can find all that information in the CIA report."

"CIA is not sharing that report with the navy or any other service," Sally informs. "But they did provide two names to NIS that might need investigating."

Sally turns on the tape recorder and repeats her last question. "When did you have the discussion and what did Bella Heinzler tell you about Robert Sweeney?"

"The first time was on a train several hours before I delivered her to the CIA in Italy. Bella told me that Sweeney was not one of her espionage targets. She said that she and Sweeney had a romantic relationship for about one year when she worked undercover in

Dunoon, Scotland during the early 1970s. Bella said she never attempted to extract classified information from him, and to the best of her knowledge he never accidently mentioned any classified information to her.

"The second time we talked about Sweeney was the night before the CIA took her into the defector protection program. She said that she told the CIA interrogators everything she knew about Robert Sweeney which included her assertion that Sweeney was just a love interest. She worried that he might be arrested by American authorities and she felt guilty that he would be charged for something that he was not guilty. She emphasized that she did not manipulate him for secrets and they rarely talked about his work. When I asked her what he did in the navy, she said he managed boat traffic in the loch where the submarine tender was anchored. That is all I remember about our conversations regarding Robert Sweeney."

Sally shuffles some more papers; then, she asks, "Did you and Bella Heinzler ever discuss a U.S. Navy Petty Officer named Donald Woodall?"

"Yes," Rig answers. "Bella talked about him during the same two occurrences she talked about Robert Sweeney. She admitted that Woodall was a specified target for extracting classified information. She said he never provided any classified information. She gave up trying to extract classified information from Woodall. She departed La Maddalena while he was at sea and never contacted him again. She holds the same guilt about Woodall that she holds for Sweeney. That's all she said about Woodall."

Sally turns off the tape recorder. Then, she comments, "From what you say, Bella Heinzler has a conscience. Does she?"

"Yes," Rig affirms. "She also has a big heart. She donated time and money to orphanages, and she was a counselor to young girls.

"Bella became the victim of a corrupt organization. When she joined the European Communist Alliance, she thought she was joining a cause for the betterment of Europe. Then, some years ago, she began uncovering bits of evidence showing corruption at high levels of The Communist Alliance. She was investigating the murder of an associate in La Maddalena when she uncovered directors in The Communist Alliance were selling illegal weapons to terrorist organizations.

"Her directors became suspicious that she knew about their illegal weapons sales. Eventually, those directors set a plan to destroy her when she became involved with me. When they tried to kill us in that beach house in Italy, she became motivated to defect."

Sally responds, "You fell in love with her, right?"

Rig glances at the recorder to make sure that it is turned off. Then, he casts a thoughtful stare at Sally while he considers how to answer, but she relieves him from answering.

"Forget I asked that question," Sally says apologetically. "What I need affirmed is that our relationship has not changed. I worry about that."

"My feelings toward you have never changed," Rig says lovingly. "I appreciate your love and passion for our special relationship."

Sally comes from around her desk and plants a soft kiss on his lips. She returns to her chair.

Sally explains, "Admiral Watson has ordered that you be given a soft duty assignment. He said you need a rest. He told me that you asked for something soft."

"Yes, I did," Rig affirms. "I need a break from

fighting the evil in the world. I never thought they could wear me out, but they have."

Sally opens another file. She explains, "ONI needs a counterespionage operative in San Diego. It's a 'temp position—about six months—*find and surveil only* missions—no close contact with the bad guys. You will be substituting for an operative who is recovering from a broken leg."

"Well, that is soft," Rig admits. His tone suggests disappointment.

Sally detects disappointment in Rig's manner. She asks, "Were you expecting a position in support and administration."

"No, not at all. I just don't want this to be my first step out of hardline field missions. I know what happens to field operatives as they approach forty."

"You're only thirty-three," Sally responds dismissively and with a chuckle.

Rig realizes he is being silly and casts a sheepish smile. He asks, "Who will be my controller?"

"Jeff Borden. He's a GS-12 with ten-years of experience in naval intelligence. He's been in San Diego for six years."

"I've heard of him," Rig states. "Do you know

my mission orders?"

"I talked with Jeff over AUTOSEVOCOM. He said that your focus will be Point Loma. Your cover assignment is an instructor at the Radioman Schools."

Rig expresses contemplation. He says, "I've never been to Instructor School."

Sally pushes a large book across the desk toward Rig and says, "You should read this before you report."

Rig stares at the book's title: *"Navy Instructor Manual"*

"When do I report?"

"Next week. I will get started on your orders. Your record will show that you attended Instructor School in the distant past."

Rig asks, "Can I have Jeff's AUTOSEVOCOM number? I want to talk to him about my assignment."

"His number is in the mission file, along with some official messages and details about the check-in process."

Sally walks out of the office.

Rig picks up the handset on the red-colored AUTOSEVOCOM phone set.

4

Santa Monica Film Festival
Hotel Grand Marquis
Santa Monica, California

Billionaire businessman and movie producer Werner Braune sits on the convention hall stage with TV news interviewer, Elizabeth 'Betsy' Winger. The stage is arranged in talk show design. A small audience of movie industry celebrities and renowned movie directors stare up at the stage.

Werner Braune is famous worldwide for his business empire that includes the international movie industry. His slim frame, perfectly shaped gray hair, piercing blue eyes, and sophisticated manner presents a commanding image. A polished English accent enhances his suave persona. Whenever he is present, he is the center of attention; and all present instinctively fall subservient to him.

The TV network interviewer is famous nationwide for her interviews of powerful people. She is a veteran investigative journalist with 25-years of experience in TV news.

"Mr. Braune, surveys of festival participants say your latest film, *Last Flag Standing*, will win the award for best movie at this festival and at the Academy Awards."

"I am not surprised." Braune responds. "*Last Flag Standing* is a quality film in all categories."

Betsy Winger, the interviewer, casts a curious expression at Braune as she asks, "What do you say to the critics who claim your film is the most anti-America movie ever made in America. They say your portrayal of America as an evil force in the world is so convincing that both American and foreign audiences cheer as the American Flag falls into the mud at the end . . . when the American military is finally defeated by the armed forces of *The World Confederation*."

Braune responds dispassionately, "It's futuristic fiction; it's entertainment."

"Futuristic?" Betsy questions. "The story takes place 50 years from now, the year 2030. Your critics say it is a political warning of a coming new order, predicting an authoritarian world government."

Braune retorts, "In the Star Trek movies, earth has a single world government—*United Earth*. No one ever criticizes that."

Betsy continues, "*Last Flag Standing* paints American patriots as uneducated psychotic bigots not worthy of civilized considerations. Your *World Confederation Army* mows down American patriots in the same manner as a *take no prisoners* vendetta."

"Not my armies—it's fiction," Braune affirms.

"In the movie, *World Confederation* leaders denounce the existence of country flags, proclaiming country flags promote nationalism. The *World Confederation* outlawed the manufacture and display of national flags. After the American Flag fell at the end of the movie, the *World Confederation Flag* was raised."

"Fiction," Braune states firmly in an even tone.

Betsy informs, "American conservatives and their organizations are denouncing the film as anti-American and fascist propaganda; while leading American socialists praise the film."

"I am a film maker," Braune affirms, "not a political activist."

Soft applause arises from the audience.

Betsy pauses to announce a change in tone. She asks, "The popularity of *Last Flag Standing* says sequel. Is there a sequel in the works?"

"Always a possibility but no discussion of a sequel at this time."

Betsy asks a few more questions about previous movies made by Braune; then, the interview terminates.

As Braune departs the conference hall and walks toward the elevators. His two bodyguards clear the way. He ignores questions from fans and reporters. Braune and his bodyguards take the elevator to the top floor.

Braune enters the living room of his five room suite. His VP for Special Projects hands him a glass with two shots of Irish whiskey.

Braune looks toward the door leading to the master bedroom. He asks, "Are we alone?"

"Yes."

"When was the last time the suite was swept for surveillance devices?"

"This afternoon. We are free to talk."

"Betsy followed the script perfectly," Braune states in a pleased tone. "You can deposit half the agreed amount into her Swiss account. Deposit the other half after that interview airs on her network. According to her, that will be tomorrow night's news broadcast. Televising that interview on national TV should draw an additional two-million viewers into theaters."

"Okay. I'll take care of it," the VP promises. Then, he informs, "Bill Owens is in the hotel coffee shop, waiting to see you."

"Are we sure Owens was not followed?"

"Our security team escorted him here; they engaged anti-surveillance protocols. They were not followed."

"Okay, have one man from the security detail sneak Owens up here."

While Braune waits for Owens, he sits in an overstuffed chair and sips Irish whiskey. He reviews his association with Owens.

Bill Owens directs Braune's west coast operation to sabotage the Reagan campaign. When Owens was recommended to Braune by one of *The Trajan Consortium* directors, Braune had Owens investigated. The name *Bill Owens* is fake. But, then, all the American political operatives he employs operate under aliases.

Bill Owens enters the suite. As usual, he is dressed and groomed conservatively in a grey suit and highly polished shoes.

Owens and Werner Braune sit in stuffed chairs, facing each other across an ornate coffee table.

"I need money for research and investigations. So I can dig deeper into Reagan's past."

"How much?"

"One-hundred-thousand dollars."

"Okay. I will deposit tomorrow."

Owens expresses astonishment.

"There will be more if you need it. I want a weekly expenditure report and operations report."

"Yes, of course," Owens replies in an agreeable tone.

5

San Diego

Rig arrives at the airport early evening. He picks up his rental car from the Avis counter; then drives directly to the Naval Training Center located on Point Loma.

At the Rosecrans gate, the gate sentry directs Rig to the Staff Personnel Office where he will be instructed further.

Rig checks in with the duty personnelman who takes his records and hands him a check-in sheet. Rig turns down the offer for a room in the chiefs barracks.

Thirty minutes later, Rig opens the door to a top floor apartment in Ocean Beach. The San Diego ONI office maintains the fully furnished apartment that includes a supply of dishes, towels, and linens.

Rig drops his suitcases in the middle of the living room; then takes a tour of the one-bedroom apartment. He starts with the balcony located off the living room. The balcony provides a clear view of the beach two-blocks away and of the setting sun on the ocean's horizon. He sees a grocery store on the next block and is reminded to get something for tonight's dinner.

In the bedroom he slides open the closet door. A supply of clothes hangers dangle from the rod. He puts his hand on a clothes hook, turns it ninety-degrees, and slides it one inch toward the wall. A "click" announces the unlocking of the weapons locker. A six-foot-high by two-foot-wide section of the closet wall swings open. The weapons locker is six inches deep and empty. Rig is not surprised because he was told he would not be issued weapons for his mission. No weapons issued is a reminder of a soft duty assignment.

Rig owns his own weapon. Years ago, ONI licensed Rig as an U.S. Armed Forces Courier to cover any situation in which he might be searched by authorities. He removes his 9mm Beretta, extra ten-round magazine, and courier credentials from the airlines security case and places them on a shelf in the weapons locker.

After stowing his clothes in drawers and the closet, he walks to the grocery store. He chooses a large roast beef deli sandwich with an extra portion of onions. For liquid refreshment, he purchases several bottles of

Perrier carbonated mineral water and a bottle of *Paul Masson Cabernet Sauvignon.*

Rig takes his groceries to the two-chair table on the apartment balcony. As he eats the sandwich and drinks the wine, he takes in the nighttime view of the beach and ocean.

Being back on American soil should have him relaxed and feeling safer than he did during the last eighteen months in Spain and Italy. But when he was stateside the last time, he unofficially and secretly engaged in battles with a vicious labor union that attacked his family in Seal Beach. So vicious that the labor union sent professional assassins to kill him.

Because of his undercover training by naval intelligence, Rig was alert and aware of his surroundings when the assassins arrived on scene. Rig put one in a coffin and permanently disabled the other who is now serving twenty years to life for the attempted murders of Rigney Page and Sally Macfurson.

Rig appreciates that ONI gave him a soft stateside assignment this time. As he stares toward the ocean, he makes a mental list of ocean sports in which he will participate.

His hometown of Seal Beach is only a two-hour drive to the north. He makes a mental note to call his parents and sisters tomorrow and schedule a visit with them for next weekend.

He eats only half of the deli sandwich, but he continues to drink the wine until half the bottle is gone. He sighs deeply and finishes the second bottle of *Perrier*.

In the bedroom, Rig stares defiantly at the bare mattress and pillows—wishing he had made the bed earlier. He feels too tired to make the bed and considers just falling on the mattress and sleep clothed.

Sensibility overcomes impulse. He makes the bed, knowing he will get a better night's sleep lying naked between soft, clean sheets.

6

Main Gate
Naval Station San Diego

Bill Owens, *The Trajan Consortium's* hired gun for west coast political sabotage, stands on the sidewalk along South 32nd Street—fifty yards north of the naval station main gate. He wears conservative style sports clothes and a navy ball cap. His apparel along with his military haircut renders him inconspicuous among the sailors who walk to and from the main gate.

As anticipated for this Sunday morning, vehicle traffic volume in and out of the gate is low and the small parking lot near the main gate is empty. The lower volume of Sunday morning traffic allows for a smaller staff of marine security guards on the gate as compared to other days of the week.

Three passenger vans with heavily tinted windows turn the corner at East Harbor Drive and South 32nd Street. The vans move toward the naval station main gate.

Owens checks his watch—9:55 AM. He

expresses satisfaction that his plan is on time.

The three passenger vans stop in the small parking lot to the right of the main gate. The vans draw the attention of the marine gate guards. Standard Operating Procedure requires them to stand fast at their assigned stations. One of the marine guards puts his hand on the telephone.

Twenty-five young men and women pour from the vans. They are dressed in casual clothes, all wearing lightweight jerseys of varying colors with varying political slogans on the back and a picture of a Jimmy Carter on the front. The group of men and women appear to be early twenties, except for their leader—a man about 40 who speaks through a megaphone.

The men have short haircuts, portraying they are all military; but they are not all military.

Owens focuses on the real sailors in the group—four men and one woman. All the jerseys were paid for and provided by Owens. The jerseys worn by the five sailors include a small, inconspicuous symbol that only their jerseys have. The five sailors are demonstrating for a cause and do not know that the other demonstrators in their group are civilians paid by Owens.

Satisfied that the targets are sufficiently identifiable, Owens waits for the next phase to begin.

The demonstrators march in a circle to the right side of the main gate. They carry signs and banners and chant their message.

The demonstration leader speaks through a megaphone: *"What do we want?!"*

Demonstrators shout out: *"Military union!"*

Leader: *"When do we want it?!"*

Followers: *"Now!"*

The slogans on the signs they carry display a similar message: MILITARY UNFAIR! or UNIONIZE NOW!

Owens looks at his watch. The next phase of his plan should start in one minute. He looks toward the intersection of East Harbor Drive and South 32nd Street.

A panel van with a local TV Station call letters on the side turns the intersection and moves toward the main gate. The van stops fifty-feet to the north of the marching demonstrators. A man pops out of an opening in the van's roof and sets a movie camera with tripod on the roof. The cameraman films the demonstrators, ensuring he captures the naval station sign and marine guards in the background.

The marine guards at the navy station main gate look on. The guard supervisor calls the security office to report the incident.

The cameraman signals to the demonstrators' leader to move the marchers a few feet to the left.

The leader complies with the cameraman's signal and moves the marchers closer to the naval station sign.

The cameraman speaks to the TV van driver. The van moves a few feet closer to the marchers.

A TV reporter with a microphone steps out of the van and places himself halfway the distance between the TV van and the marchers. The naval station sign, the reporter, and the demonstrators are all caught in the camera's view.

Owens's assistant had obtained the cooperation of the TV station when he promised a hot, exclusive story. The TV employees know the demonstration is staged, but they do not know what is coming next.

A crowd of off-duty sailors has gathered in the area where Owens stands. All of them stare with interest at the pro-union demonstrators.

Owens turns and faces the intersection. He touches the bill of his ball cap twice.

The pro-union demonstrators continue their chant.

The TV reporter approaches the demonstration leader, hoping for an interview.

A group of thuggish-looking men, all handpicked and paid by Bill Owens, turn the corner at the intersection and move quickly toward the naval station main gate. They carry signs with messages opposing military unions.

Owens supplied the thugs' political wear, which include pictures of Ronald Reagan printed on the front. Owens had several of the thugs remove the sleeves from their jerseys so that their iron crosses, swastikas, and demon tattoos are easily visible. All the thugs' jerseys have the American Flag printed on the back.

The thugs' signs were also designed by Owens. Some of their signs proclaim UNIONISM IS EXTORTION and others declare NO UNION PANSIES IN THE MILITARY and a couple other signs warned UNIONS DESTROY DISCIPLINE.

The sign staffs of both groups were designed to Owens's specifications. The sign staffs carried by the thugs' are made of walnut wood. The sign staffs carried by the pro-union demonstrators are made of pine wood.

When the pro-union demonstrators see the thugs coming their way, they stop marching and express anxiety. But only the five sailors are worried. The paid members of the pro-union demonstrators are part of this staged event and previously rehearsed what happens next when the real sailors were absent.

When the group of thugs is ten-feet away from the pro-union demonstrators, the thugs start yelling insults at the pro-union demonstrators, calling them "unmilitary" and "undisciplined pussies" who want a union.

The thugs penetrate the perimeter of the pro-union demonstrators and begin shoving the pro-union demonstrators. Fists are raised. Walnut sign staffs are punched into the stomachs of the five sailors and then walnut staffs tap the sailors on the head. The taps to the head are strong enough to render the sailors unconscious but not strong enough to do permanent harm.

As the sailors fall, the thugs turn and run toward the intersection; they carry their signs with them. At the same time, the conscious pro-union demonstrators pile back into the passenger vans.

The passenger vans speed off.

The five sailors remain unconscious in the traffic lanes.

The TV station camera captures it all.

Beyond the view of the naval station main gate, the thugs climb into a tour bus parked on East Harbor Drive.

Bill Owens departs the scene.

At the naval station main gate. Members of the TV crew are exuberant over their film recording of political *thugs* attacking a group of pro-union sailors.

The TV reporter moves toward the demonstrators laying on the ground. At the same time several marine guards approach the downed sailors. The cameraman captures it all.

Two of the sailors are sitting up and holding their heads. Blood seeps from their wounds.

"They're all breathing!" reports one of the marine guards.

Naval Station Police vehicles arrive on scene. They close off all but one in-lane and one out-lane.

Telephone reports begin climbing the naval station chain of command.

The TV crew remains on scene and captures all events including the removal of the injured sailors by medical personal and the beginning of the Naval Investigative Service questioning of witnesses.

Later in the day at the top of the local evening news, the TV reporter who was at the demonstration leads with a news alert: "REAGAN FASCISTS BRUTALLY BEAT PEACEFUL DEMONSTRATORS AT THE SAN DIEGO NAVAL STATION. DETAILED REPORT AND FILM TO FOLLOW."

The broadcasted film provides clear political separation between the two groups by capturing the political jerseys. The film also clearly shows the Nazi symbol tattoos on the thugs' arms. The thugs hitting the pro-union demonstrators with sign staffs is clear and distinct.

The national TV networks pick up the film and broadcast the story nationwide. TV news contributors add anti-Reagan opinions to what they are calling the *San Diego Riot*.

Large city newspapers publish opinions written by their employees. Those opinions demand that Ronald Reagan be held accountable for not preventing his fascist followers from committing acts of violence.

The Reagan campaign denies association with the *San Diego rioters* and denounces violence.

7

Naval Training Center
San Diego, California

Rig drives his rental car through the NTC Rosecrans gate; then, he searches for instructor parking near the Radioman Schools building. He finds an open spot in the chief petty officers section of a parking lot across the street to the Radioman Schools building.

The morning is warm and sunny; he wears pilot sunglasses to protect his eyes from the glare of the sun. His Summer White uniform accents his tall athletic physique, which draws stares from those passing by. The short sleeves reveal his heavily muscled and thickly haired forearms. He wears his Surface Warfare insignia above his ribbons and his Submarine Warfare insignia below his ribbons because he will be teaching in the surface navy Radioman Schools.

As he crosses the intersection, he glances to his left in an effort to see the Recruit Training Command that is located several blocks away. Seeing the RTC gate a few blocks away brings back memories of his boot camp experience fifteen-years ago.

Rig removes his sunglasses as he enters the main entrance of the Navy Radioman Schools building. He walks to the quarterdeck counter and informs the watch, "I am Senior Chief Page, I am reporting aboard for instructor duty."

A surprised expression appears on the quarterdeck watch's face. He stares at Rig's face. "I know you, Senior Chief. We were stationed at San Miguel together. I worked in receivers."

Rig's memory searches back five years to when he was undercover at NAVCOMMSTA San Miguel Philippines.

The quarter deck watch wears Service Dress White uniform—black neckerchief and ribbons. His left sleeve displays a First Class Radioman chevron and one hash mark. His nametag says *Carpenter*. Rig remembers the face and remembers engaging in work related activities with this radioman.

"I remember you," Rig responds.

"Do you remember signing off some of my practical factors?"

"Yes. I remember," Rig responds.

"I was there when you were in that car accident and medivac'd back to the states. Everyone thought you were seriously injured, but then we all read about you in the *Navy Times* just a few months later about defeating a terrorist attack on the base you were at. They called you a hero. Was the *Navy Times* correct about all that?"

"Yes," Rig answers. "The Navy Times provided an accurate account of what happened."

"I was pleased—we were all pleased—to see that you recovered well from the car accident."

"Thank you," Rig responds sincerely. "How long were you there after I departed?"

"One year," Carpenter answers.

"How long have you been here?" Rig asks.

"Six months." Carpenter pauses, expressing that something has come to mind. "Hey, Senior, I would like to buy you a couple of drinks after work at the Acey-Deucey Club. We can talk over old times, and I can brief you on who's who and what's what at Radioman Schools. Is that, okay?"

"I would like that," Rig replies sincerely, "but I am booked up today and tomorrow.

Wednesday evening is open."

Carpenter offers, "I work part-time at the Acey-Deucey Club. My shift starts at twenty-one-hundred. How about we meet in the club lobby on Wednesday at nineteen-hundred?"

"I will be there, looking forward to it," Rig replies with enthusiasm. He glances at the passageway that leads off the quarterdeck; he asks, "Where do I check in?"

Carpenter points to the passageway entrance and says, "Admin office is second on left."

Rig spends twenty minutes going through the check-in processes with the yeoman. Then, he is routed to the Director, Radioman Schools office for a check-in interview.

The Director, Lieutenant Commander Randolph Peterson, is a Limited Duty Officer who was selected for the LDO program ten-years ago when he was a first class radioman. The slim, medium-height officer stands up from behind his desk stretches out his arm to shake Rig's hand.

The officer glances at Rig's chest candy. A Navy Achievement medal with no stars is in priority position. The officer is impressed when he sees that Rig wears both surface and

51

submarine warfare pins.

Rig has earned more navy awards than what ONI allows him to wear. He has two Bronze Stars for Valor, awarded secretly and not allowed to be displayed on his chest. He also has three additional Navy Achievement awards, but ONI does not allow him to display the stars. ONI reasons that Rig's physical appearance and publicized *"Hero of Thurso"* past presents a powerful image that makes him a standout in any navy crowd. Having to answer a lot of questions about valor and achievement is too much attention.

After they shake hands, Commander Peterson directs Rig to take the seat in front of the desk.

They sit down and face each other across the desk.

The commander specifies, "Before we can talk about your duties, I need to know your date of rank."

"July 1978."

Peterson looks down at a list of names in order by rank and then by date of rank. He frowns at what he discovers.

Rig asks, "Is there a problem, sir?"

"You are filling a first class billet. I have

never seen BUPERS do that before. I have seen assignment by one grade above the billet rank, but never two grades higher. Your date of rank makes you second senior enlisted man on the staff—junior only to Master Chief Moore.

"When I called BUPERS and asked the detailer why an E8 was assigned to an E6 billet, he told me that assigning two paygrades above billet grade is rare and against standing orders. In your case, someone high up the chain of command directed your assignment."

"Is there is a problem with my seniority?" Rig asks in a curious tone.

"By date of rank, you should be assigned as senior instructor. However, Senior Chief Brazinski is assigned as senior instructor by billet; he is next senior to you and has one year in grade. If I moved you into the senior instructor position, half a dozen chiefs move down the position order. It's a morale issue, and one that I would like to avoid."

Rig, also, wants to avoid controversy and morale issues. He does not want to draw attention to himself. Rig asks, "What would you like to do, sir?"

"I would like you to lead the Curriculum Development Section. You would supervise the work of one chief and three first class. You would not teach classes nor would you be assigned to a duty section."

Rig likes the commander's proposal. With no commitment to teaching daily classes and not being required to stand duty, he would have more time to spend on his naval intelligence tasks.

Rig responds with smile on his face. "I'm okay with that, sir."

Commander Peterson smiles back and says, "Good. As leader of curriculum development, you report directly to me. You and I, the OICs of each school, and the master chief will meet weekly."

"OICs?" Rig questions.

Lieutenant Mancini is the OIC Radioman 'A' School, and Lieutenant Braun is the OIC for Radioman 'C' School."

"LDOs?" Rig asks.

"Yes. Both of them. Is that important?"

"When disagreement arises over technical details in draft curriculum, I tend to respect the argument of those who actually worked in the radioman rating over those who have not."

"Are you expecting disagreements over technical details?" the Director asks.

"Are there not currently disagreements over technical details in draft curriculum?"

Commander Peterson expresses amusement as he asks, "How did you know?"

"Because disagreement over how and why things are done, radioman wise, occurred at every command I was stationed."

"How were such disagreements settled?" Peterson asks.

Rig explains, "If I were involved in the disagreement, I would produce the manual or directive relevant to the subject and whatever the manual or directive specified settled the disagreement."

"Senior Chief, I think you and I will get along just fine."

8

Hilton Strand Hotel
Los Angeles, California

Bill Owens enters the five-star Hilton Strand Hotel, crosses the lobby, and enters an empty elevator. He selects the top floor. He has a 2:00 PM appointment with TV news journalist and celebrity interviewer, Elizabeth 'Betsy' Winger.

Owens wears a light gray, three-piece suit. To enhance his current, false conservative persona, his brown hair is cut short and his face is clean shaven.

Owens knocks on the door of the hotel suite.

A young woman opens the door.

Owens recognizes the young woman as one of Betsy Winger's assistants.

The young woman leads Owens into the suite's sitting room.

Betsy Winger sits at a table and types on an IBM Selectric. She stops typing when she sees Owens enter the room.

Betsy stands and tells her assistant, "Ann, take a break, about thirty minutes."

Ann departs the suite.

Betsy points to an overstuffed chair and says, "Take a seat, Bill."

Owens sits.

Betsy sits on a settee across the coffee table from Owens. She does not offer any refreshments. Although Werner Braune arranged this meeting, she wants this meeting to be short. She does not like Bill Owens and feels uncomfortable being around him.

"What do you have for me?" Betsy asks.

"More of the same," Owens states. He hands her a thick envelope.

Betsy opens the envelope and reads drafts of news articles. The drafts contain accusations of Reagan and members of his senior staff committing various nefarious acts. Authenticity is provided by citing '*anonymous Reagan campaign staffers that fear retribution.*'

While Betsy reads the drafts, Owens evaluates the third-highest rated journalist in American TV. At age 50, Betsy Winger maintains a slim figure and projects an attractive professional image. Her renowned confidence and power usually intimidates others of lower status. However, Owens is neither intimidated nor impressed. She is not above misrepresenting facts for a sensational story or a political objective. Owens's views her as just another political operative like him.

Betsy advises, "We have already published a lot of these anonymous accusations. Too many could result in lack of credibility."

Owens dismisses Betsy's assessment. "Anything with your byline radiates credibility. Both Werner and his analysts believe that."

Like Braune and Owens, Betsy is willing to engage in corrupt and immoral acts to prevent Ronald Reagan from becoming president. But she knows too many unsubstantiated accusations can damage her image.

"Okay," Betsy responds. "I air the three most damaging of these in my broadcasts this week and I will pass them on to city newspapers. With multiple news organizations publishing these accusations, the public will believe the information comes from multiple sources. A perception of multiple sources adds credibility."

"What about the rest of them?" Owens asks in a challenging tone.

"I will spread them out over the next month. Tell Werner he must trust me on this."

Ann, Betsy's assistant, enters the room.

Betsy stands, indicating the meeting is over.

9

Task Force 152 Field Office
Naval Base San Diego

Jeff Borden hands Rig a three-ring binder.

Rig opens the binder and turns some of the pages. The binder contains photographs of people exiting what appears to be restaurants or nightclubs.

"Those seven people are your targets. Your predecessor had just identified them as suspicious characters in the Point Loma area. We do not have full names and addresses. Everything we know about each of them is typed on pages behind their pictures.

"They frequent bars and clubs in the Point Loma area and establish relationships with sailors. A list of their haunts is listed on the back of their photographs."

Rig fingers through the photographs, scanning their photos and list of haunts. He comments, "There are both men and women in this binder."

"Sailors vulnerable to extortion by foreign agents come in all shapes, sizes, genders, mindsets, and sexual orientation."

Rig nods and exhibits agreement.

Borden instructs, "You should watch one haunt each night, randomly, Wednesday through Saturday. Watch the haunt from outside. Avoid contact with those suspects and avoid going inside those haunts. When you see a suspect leave a haunt with a sailor, tail them. Plant radio beacons on both their cars. Obtain addresses and car license plates of both the suspect and the sailor. No more than that. Once you have that information your mission regarding that suspect is complete. ONI Surveillance Specialists will take over after that.

"I will provide you with all the equipment you need. You must wear a disguise when out watching haunts and tailing suspects. I will provide your disguise. We will make you look like a long-haired civilian.

"We have an apartment in a building with an underground gated garage. There will be a car in that garage registered to your alias disguise. There is also a separate car space reserved for your own car. That apartment is where you will change into your disguise to include a photo ID and driver's license that matches your disguise alias. Multiple operatives use that apartment to change in and out of their disguises. So don't be surprised when you encounter others in that apartment."

Rig asks, "When do I start?"

"We need five more days to finish up some details and fit you for your disguise. Start next Tuesday."

10

Acey-Deucey Club
Naval Training Center San Diego

Most large naval installations have three nightclub-restaurant type facilities for enlisted personal. The Enlisted Club serves E-4 and below. The Acey-Deucy Club serves First and Second Class Petty Officers (E-5 & E-6)—also known as The Petty Officers Club. The Chiefs Club serves all chief ranks.

As Rig enters the front entrance of the Acey-Deucey Club, he sees Petty Officer Carpenter standing in the center of the lobby and glancing at his watch. Both men wear casual civilian clothes.

Rig apologizes for being ten-minutes late.

"No problem," Carpenter states. "I was five-minutes late myself."

Carpenter leads the way into the barroom. The barroom is the size of a basketball court and includes a dance floor that takes up one-third of the barroom's space. A small stage stands at the far end of the dancefloor. The serving bar is thirty-barstools long with two bartenders serving. Tables and chairs populate all remaining floorspace.

Rig quickly calculates about 90 people in the barroom with the men-to-women ratio about 2 to 1. Most of patrons crowd around the serving bar. Every barstool is occupied.

Country music flows at moderate volume from the sound system.

Carpenter leads them to a table near the dancefloor and away for the crowd.

A waiter arrives at the table. They both agree to a pitcher of draft beer.

Rig scans the room again. "More women in here than I expected."

"It's ladies night," Carpenter explains. "Women drink for free. This place will be partying by twenty-one-hundred, and there will be three-times the number of women."

"Free drinks draw in that many women?"

"Actually, Senior, this place is packed mostly every night, and there is always a lot of women. Free drinks on ladies night draw in more than usual."

Rig is staring toward the serving bar when a slender woman wearing tight black slacks and a tight, cleavage-exposing black pullover enters the barroom. She wears her jet-black hair with long curls flowing to her shoulders Her dark red lipstick contrasts brightly against her pale colored skin and her eyes that are heavy with dark makeup. Rig recognizes her from the photo binder that his ONI controller gave him yesterday. He does not remember any of the pictures listing the Acey-Deucey Club as a frequent haunt. He continues to stare at the woman while considering what he should do. He has been taken by surprise.

Carpenter notices that Rig's attention is drawn to the serving bar. He asks, "What is it, Senior?"

Rig continues to watch the hip-swaying woman walk slowly along the line of barstools looking for an empty seat. He remembers that Carpenter works part-time in this club and can be a source of information. "Do you know the lady in black?"

"That's Cleo," Carpenter responds. "She comes in her three, four nights a week. Are you interested?"

"What do you know about her?" Rig inquires.

"Well, she was dating a radioman attending C7 school. They often met here. They would have a drink or two; then they would leave together. That radioman graduated a few weeks ago and transferred.

A sailor offers Cleo his barstool. Sailors flock around her, but she appears not to be interested.

Carpenter adds, "Since her radioman boyfriend transferred, she now leaves the club alone."

"Is she navy?"

"No, a civilian."

"How does she get on base," Rig asks.

"Probably with a club pass issued by the club manager. Like a lot of the civilian women who are in here now, they show their club pass at the main gate and sign in by logging their drivers' license and car license plate. Then, they get a temporary restricted base pass that allows them to drive directly from the main gate to the club. As I look around the room, I recognize most of the women as regulars. They're either single civilians like I explained or they're dependent wives who are WESTPAC widows. I only see one woman who I know is in the navy."

"Well, I can see how that would be good for sailors' morale," Rig acknowledges. Then, he questions, "No security problems, then?"

"I think if there were security problems, the practice would be suspended. I am told that the club pass has been around for decades. Like you said, it's good for morale. The Enlisted Club and the Chiefs Club do the same. But this place is the most popular."

Rig asks, "What's the club's policy on chiefs coming in here alone . . . without a petty officer escort?"

"As long as the chief is in civilian clothes, management allows it. Not many chiefs come in here, though."

For the next hour, Rig and Carpenter discuss their adventures in the Philippines. Rig asks Carpenter about the current location of some of the sailors who worked in the Communications Center—the division Rig supervised.

Rig observes the lady in black, Cleo, slip off her barstool and walk toward the lobby.

"Excuse me," Rig tells Carpenter. "I need to go to the head."

Rig steps into the lobby. He does not see her. He glances toward the front entrance glass doors and sees her walking toward the parking lot.

He does not follow her outside for concern

she might notice him. He remembers the warning from his controller to avoid contact with suspects.

Cleo enters the driver's side of a midsize sedan.

Rig plans to walk out to the curb of the parking lot as she drives by. But the car does not move.

The car's rear is toward the club. Rig considers he might be able to sneak close enough to read her car's license plate.

She would need to be looking in the rearview mirror at an angle to see me, he concludes.

A young man in civilian clothes and carrying a gym bag enters the passenger side of Cleo's car.

A puff of smoke from the exhaust alerts that the car has been started. The car must pass in front of the club to enter the main street. Rig walks out the door and goes to the sidewalk. He leans against a light post, his back toward the direction the car must come. He lowers his head but looks toward the direction where he can read the license plate when the car passes by. He speculates that Cleo and her companion will not pay much attention to him, if any

As the car passes, Rig memorizes the license plate number on the rear of the car.

After the car turns onto the main street and is out of sight, Rig enters the club and goes directly to the men's head. He pulls a pen from his pocket, pulls a paper towel from the dispenser, and writes the license number on the towel.

Rig returns to the barroom and continues his conversation with Carpenter.

11

Venice Beach
Los Angeles, California

Bill Owens parks his car in a public lot one block away from the Venice Beach Boardwalk. The afternoon sun shines brightly and warms the air enough to allow wearing a lightweight shirt and trousers. He walks quickly toward the appointment location.

Owens's research team uncovered one of Ronald Reagan's girlfriends from the 1930s who might be willing to engage in a plot of political sabotage. During their only telephone conversation, Cassandra Reynolds refused to talk about her relationship with Ronald Reagan. Owens enticed a meeting by offering her three-hundred dollars just to show up for meeting. He knows she is desperate for money. He suggested a meeting in a rented conference room in his hotel. She refused to meet him in a private setting but said she would meet with him in a public setting. They agreed to a bench on the Venice Beach Boardwalk. She lives in a shared apartment that is a fifteen-minute bus ride from the boardwalk.

Owens knows that Cassandra Reynolds is an ageing bit-player in movies and television. When she was younger, she was in high demand as a bit-player because of her figure and beauty but never as leading actress because her talent did not meet the standard. As her looks aged, her bit parts become those of mother or aunt and then finally as grandmother. Owens knows that offers for acting parts are much less frequent now than when she was younger. Her bank statements show that her life savings is dwindling; her social security checks do not cover her basic needs.

Cassandra was married twice; her husbands divorced her because of her infidelity. The infidelity was evident; so, she made deals not to contest the divorces if the records were sealed. The only information made public was the divorce decrees by the judges. Her public reputation remains positive.

The boardwalk is not busy on this weekday afternoon. Seagulls caw overhead. The beach is not crowded and beach blankets are far apart on the sand.

As Owens approaches the bench described

by Cassandra, he sees her sitting on the bench with an expression of anticipation on her face.

When Cassandra sees a man of undistinguished manner approaching her who is dressed as Owens described on the phone, she slides as tight as she can against the bench armrest.

Owens sits in the middle of the bench. He quickly appraises the woman's appearance. She wears sunglasses and heavy makeup to hide the winkles in her face. Her hair is dyed brown. She wears a loose fitting, dark-brown pantsuit. Her shoes are quality made but worn. She is attempting to look much younger that her sixty-nine years but is failing in that attempt.

"You are Cassandra Reynolds?"

Cassandra stares at Owens and attempts to judge his manner by his appearance.

Owens presents a clean-cut appearance with short-hair, a clean-shaven face, and conservative style sports clothes.

Cassandra relaxes now that she sees that the man on the phone with a deep controlling voice is an unintimidating, medium-height, clean-cut man in his thirties.

She scans the area around her. No one is paying attention to them.

"Yes I am Cassandra. Are you Bill Owens?"

"Yes I am. May I ask you some questions?" Owens casts a reassuring smile.

"You said you would pay me three-hundred dollars just for coming to this meeting."

Owens pulls six fifty-dollar bills from his left breast pocket. He hands her the money.

Cassandra grabs the money; then, stuffs the money into her purse.

Owens pulls a bundle of one-hundred dollar bills from his right breast pocket. He proposes, "I would like to ask you some questions. I already know the answer to some of them. If you answer truthfully, I will give you another fifteen-hundred dollars. I will ask you some questions regarding your relationship with Ronald Reagan. Are you willing to continue?"

Cassandra stares hungrily at the bundle of bills.

"Ask your questions." Cassandra is committed to answering honestly.

"When did you first become friends with Ronald Reagan?"

"During the late 1930s—right after I came to Hollywood."

Owens nods. "What was your relationship with him?"

72

"We were contract players at the same movie studio and we were in the same social circle. We went out on a few dates."

"Are there people who can verify that you and Reagan were in the same social circle and dated?"

"Yes. And I have photographs."

"Were you and Reagan intimate?"

"No."

"Were you ever alone with Reagan in his home?"

"Yes."

"Why did you and Reagan stop dating?"

"Ronnie and I argued a lot about politics. We were on opposite sides and we could not set it aside."

"What was his politics?"

"He's a fascist."

"You were a registered communist, correct?"

"Yes, but no longer. I am reregistered as an independent."

"Why did you reregister as an independent?"

"Fear of losing movie roles."

"Are you going to vote for Reagan in the general election?"

"Of course not!" Cassandra hisses venomously. "He's a fascist!"

"You were in the hospital for three week during February 1939. What was the reason?"

"I fell down some steps in my apartment building. I suffered a fractured jaw, a broken forearm, and cuts and bruises."

Owens is satisfied that she has been truthful so far. Now is the time to suggest she admit to something that is not true.

Owens states, "One of my sources from your old social circle said you were in the hospital because Reagan raped you. Then, he beat you up when you threatened to report the rape to the police."

So far, Cassandra had not looked at Owens while answering. But the rape accusation caused her to swing her head toward Owens and look him directly in the eyes. "That's a lie. Who told you that?"

Owens hands the fifteen one-hundred dollar bills to Cassandra. She is somewhat bewildered as to which answers earned her the money. She adds the fifteen bills to the others in her pocket book. She casts a questioning stare at Owens while wondering what comes next.

Owens offers, "There is one-hundred thousand dollars for you if you stand up and tell the American people that the rape and beating happen as I described it."

Cassandra jerks with surprise and expresses astonishment. She reflects on the conversation so far. The purpose of this meeting becomes clear to her.

Cassandra responds, "What would happen if I said yes?"

"You would be represented by a lawyer who would do all the talking. You will only need to sit beside the lawyer and say what he tells you to say."

"Would I get national exposure on television and newspapers?"

"For sure," Owens states with certainty in his tone.

Cassandra shakes her head slightly as she says, "But I cannot prove that happened, because it didn't."

"You don't need to prove it," Owens promises. "The sensationalism of the accusation is sufficient. Your lawyer will ensure you are never placed in such a position to provide proof."

"Ronnie is a powerful man. He could sue me

for defamation."

"The best legal advice says that Reagan will not sue. Anyway, talk that over with the lawyer. I can assure you that your only commitment will be to never tell anyone your accusation is false."

"But the hospital records?" Cassandra challenges.

"Those records no longer exist," Owens responds.

"You're sure?" Cassandra challenges again.

"I'm sure," Owens affirms confidently.

"When would I get the money?" Cassandra asks.

"Immediately after your first national interview on television."

Cassandra expresses thoughtfulness as she considers the offer.

"Okay. What's next?" she asks.

"You said you have pictures of you and Ronald Reagan together on dates. Is that correct?"

"Yes."

"Time is of the essence," Owens forewarns. He hands her a business card and advises, "The offer is open for three days. Contact that lawyer within the next three days."

Owens stands, indicating their meeting is over.

Cassandra asks, "Mr. Owens, I might have some questions. How do I contact you?"

"You and I will have no more contact. That lawyer will answer any questions you have."

After Owens departs, Cassandra remains sitting on the bench and contemplates the consequences of her participation in this plot. The money and sweet revenge against Ronald Reagan motivate her to participate. She concludes that only immensely powerful people have the capability to implement such a damaging plot.

Finally, she concludes, *someone will knock Ronnie and his kind off their fascist high horse.*

12

Acey-Deucey Club
Naval Training Center San Diego

At the far end of the parking lot, Rig sits in his rental car and waits for Cleo and her boyfriend to appear. Night fell thirty minutes ago; so his presence should go unnoticed.

Rig and his San Diego controller, Jeff Borden, agreed that there is high risk in Rig wearing a disguise on base because his civilian disguise has no military affiliations. He sits undisguised and in civilian clothes in his own rental car.

Borden reported that the license number on Cleo's vehicle led to her parent's home in Texas. Her parents said they had not talked with their daughter in over three years and were unaware of the license registration. Her father is a retired navy chief.

Rig's mission tonight is to attach a radio beacon to Cleo's vehicle. If she does not appear tonight, Rig is to return each evening until she does.

"Right now, placing that beacon on her car

is your number one priority," Borden directed, "but do not tail her. Wait until she has vacated her car and is out of sight before attaching the beacon. We must not risk her seeing you out of disguise."

"This is not my first time out in the cold," Rig had responded to Borden's emphatic, detailed order.

Rig turns on his portable transistor AM radio and tunes in the local oldies station. *Barbara Ann* by the *Beach Boys* blasts through the speaker. He turns the volume down low.

A base security vehicle approaches Rig's location. The vehicle is occupied by two shore patrol petty officers. The petty officer in the front passenger seat shines a flashlight at the parked cars as they drive by.

Rig decides to play conspicuous and not attempt to hide. When the flashlight finds his face, the shore patrol vehicle stops in front of Rig's car, blocking his driving path.

The flashlight beam moves to Rig's license plate. He observes that the passenger side shore patrol is calling in the license number over the radio, and the driver side shore patrol is writing the number down on a clipboard.

The security vehicle spotlight illuminates

and is turned in the direction of Rig's car.

The two shore patrol petty officers exit their vehicle. They wear Summer White uniform with shore patrol armbands covering their rating chevrons. Instead of white hats, they wear metal helmets. The one with the flashlight approaches Rig; the other stands back a few feet and holds a clipboard. Both are armed with nightsticks only.

Rig lowers the volume on his transistor radio.

"Please show me your I.D. card," the shore patrol says in a friendly tone.

As Rig reaches for his wallet, he observes the shore patrol with the clipboard writing down the number of his base sticker located on the window.

The shore patrol examines Rig's I.D. card. Then, he hands it to the shore patrol with the clipboard who writes down Rig's information.

"May I ask what's going on?" Rig inquires.

"There has been a surge of car break-ins. Have you seen anything suspicious?"

"No," Rig answers.

"How long have you been sitting here, Senior Chief?"

"About ninety-minutes," Rig answers. "I've

been waiting for my date. I think I have been stood up."

The petty officer casts a friendly smile as he says, "A senior chief waiting for a date in the Acey-Deucey Club parking lot is not a common occurrence. I must report this incident to my supervisor and must include your detailed explanation."

"I invited her to join me for drinks at the Chiefs Club," Rig explains. "She set the time and place for us to meet. She said her restricted base pass only allows her to drive from the main gate to the Acey-Deucey Club."

The shore patrol is aware of the Acey-Deucey Club restricted base pass. He nods and expresses understanding.

The other shore patrol busily writes Rig's explanation in the clipboard log.

During this questioning session, Rig has kept an eye on the parking lot, hoping Cleo does not arrive while shore patrol is present.

The shore patrol says in a friendly tone, "Thank you for your cooperation, Senior Chief."

"Anytime," Rig responds.

The two shore patrol enter their vehicle and continue their security check of the parking lot. Five minutes later, the security vehicle is out of sight.

Rig raises the volume on his transistor radio. The DJ announces that a commercial-free thirty minutes of top twenty songs from 1964 follows. He decides to stay parked for another thirty minutes.

As the songs play, he is reminded of his high school years. He remembers all the surfing, all his girlfriends, playing sports, and hanging out at the Seal Beach Café with friends.

Such wonderful times back then, he reminisces. *I was so naïve—so unworldly—so innocent. If someone told me then that I would choose a career of fighting the evil in the world, I would have said they did not understand my life's goals. How times have changed!*

Cleo does not appear.

As he starts the car, he lets out a big sigh as he craves for more adventurous and intriguing missions in Europe or WESTPAC.

13

Reno, Nevada

The Arlington Assisted Living complex sits one block south of the Truckee River in the old residential section of town. The only street access to the complex is through the administration building's main entrance.

Bill Owens walks up the four concrete steps of the main entrance and walks into the lobby. He notices one of the security cameras over the reception desk is aimed at the main entrance. He follows the directions he was given over the phone and walks through the dining room to the patio. A man in a wheel chair sits at a table; a tray of coffee sits on the table in front of him. The man wears a thick cardigan sweater and has a blanket covering his legs. As promised, Randy Gough is alone on the patio, probably because of the mid-morning chill.

Gough is a frail man who appears not to have many years left. When he sees Owens approaching, he asks, "You are Mr. Owens?"

Owens nods; then takes a chair at the small

patio table, sitting directly across from Gough.

"I had some coffee made for us; have some."

Owens says, "Thank you, Mr. Gough, for seeing me on such short notice." Owens pours himself a cup of coffee and adds some sugar.

Gough stares suspiciously at Owens and says, "You said on the phone that you would give me five-hundred dollars if I agreed to meet with you and listen to your pitch."

Owens hands Gough five one-hundred dollar bills.

Gough puts the money in his sweater pocket, then says, "Who do you want identified as belonging to the American Communist Party."

Owens expresses surprise that Gough is on target.

Gough explains, "Mr. Owens, since that infamous congressional investigation into the communist party many years ago when I betrayed my friends, people like you occasionally show up at my doorstep and offer me money just to listen to their pitch; most often during election years."

"People like me?" Owens questions.

"Yes.   Political   detectives?   Political

investigators? Political operatives? Whatever they're called these days."

In a curious tone, Owens states, "I was told that in the past you refused to meet with people like me."

"That was a long time ago. My life has change," Gough states in a defeated tone. "My heart is failing and I have been given two years at most. I must stay in this dreadful place, but with more money I can upgrade my lifestyle. I can shift from a two-man room to a private room, and I can afford some of the more comfortable amenities they offer here. So, let's see if I can give you want you want."

Owens nods and accepts Gough's motives. "My research reveals that you were working in the Hollywood movie industry as far back as the 1930s."

"Yes, yes, I was friends with Ronald Reagan back then. We were contract actors with the same movie studio. That's why you're here, right? Ronald Reagan, right?"

"Were you friends with Reagan?"

"Yes."

"Were you close friends?"

"There were about twenty of us that socialized frequently. Ronnie and I were close enough to buy each other drinks in a bar and talk like friends."

Owens explains, "I am seeking confirmation that Reagan was in the American Communist Party. Can you help me with that? And if you can, will you confirm it for nationwide publication?"

"Many in our crowd were registered communists. Some were active, like me. Back then, capitalism was not in favor with most in our crowd."

"Can you remember the names of those friends who were communists?" Anxiousness edges Owens's tone.

"I might be able to give you what you want. What must I do?"

"First, I would video tape you saying Reagan was a communist. You must list names of communists that were friends of both you and Reagan. Then I would pass that video tape around. Newspapers and network news will do the rest by spinning up accusations and presenting them as substantiated truth. Eventually you will be interviewed by a network news program. Through all of it, you will be protected by a skillful lawyer."

"I can confirm that that Ronnie had

communist friends."

"Can you name those friends of Reagan that were communists? Did Reagan know they were communists?" Owens's tone becomes enthusiastic, believing he has discovered gold.

"Look, Mr. Owens. Only a few were true communist. Many of our actor friends registered in the communist party and proclaimed their support for communism. But they were not real communists. Most of them did it for the publicity and to curry favor of average Americans who were not making the huge amounts of money that actors were earning."

Owens states, "That many actors were registered communists is what has survived the decades, but details of their motives didn't."

"To answer your question, Mr. Owens. Yes. Ronnie knew some in our circle were card carrying communists. But communism did not have the bad rep then as it does now. For the last thirty years, Ronnie has been an anti-communist activist. Attempting to paint him otherwise will be difficult."

"All the better if we can put doubts in the minds American voters," Owens responds. "The evidence I want is from the thirties and forties, before Reagan earned his reputation as a communist hater."

"Well, that might work," Gough suggests. "But before we go any further, we must discuss compensation for my exposé."

"What do you want?" Owens asks.

"I want fifty-thousand dollars. Half upon completion of your video tape interview and the remainder upon completion of taping the network news interview."

"That's excessive, Mr. Gough." Owens tone is defiant in an attempt to bargain the price. However, he knows fifty-thousand is reasonable and knows that Mr. Braune would not flinch at twice that amount.

"I doubt you will find any other communist from those times that have more notoriety and credibility than me. I have photographs and a daily journal."

"Do any of those photographs or your daily journal prove that Ronald Reagan was a communist."

"No, but they show that Reagan associated with communists. It's enough for reporters to damage Ronnie's image by speculating on what the photographs portray and citing anonymous sources for validation." Gough pauses for a moment; then states, "You won't get any better than that."

"Okay," Owens says agreeably. "We will film my interview with you in my hotel room at Bally's tomorrow afternoon. I will send a limo equipped for wheelchairs at 1:00 PM. I will meet you at Bally's front entrance."

"Okay," Gough agrees. Then, he demands, "And you will show me the twenty-five thousand dollars in cash before we start the interview. And you will give me that twenty-five thousand after you tape the interview and before I leave your room."

Owens chuckles and shakes his head. "Okay. Will do. You are not the trusting type; are you?"

"This is not my first rodeo," Gough responds in a flat, serious tone.

14

Seattle, Washington

Bill Owens stands on the roof of the five-story apartment building. Using binoculars, he scans a strip mall located across the street. Traffic is nearly nonexistent on this Sunday afternoon in this suburb of mostly brownstone apartment buildings and small businesses.

Owens's target is the Jimmy Carter campaign office on the end of the twelve-store strip mall. The sign on the door says "CLOSED" with working hours listed as Monday through Saturday.

Through binoculars, Owens watches his associate walk to front door of the campaign office.

The associate tests the door latch—locked. He knocks on the door. No one responds. The associate steps to the center of the sidewalk, looks up toward Owens, then exhibits the okay sign with his hand.

Owens opens a briefcase and pulls out a handheld radio. He presses the transmit button and speaks into the radio, "Begin the protest."

Four blocks away in a rented tour bus, the same leader who led the pro-union demonstrators at the San Diego Naval Station speaks into the handheld radio, "Acknowledged."

"Go," the leader tells the driver.

Several minutes later, the bus enters the strip mall parking lot and parks 100 feet distant from the Carter campaign office.

Owens's associate, the one who had checked the door of the office to ensure no one was inside, enters a phone booth and calls a local TV news office.

Fifteen protesters exit the bus and form a marching circle in front of the campaign office. They carry signs that read:

"JIMMY CARTER BETRAYED AMERICA"

"PANAMA CANAL BELONGS TO AMERICA"

"AMERICA FOR AMERICANS"

"ATTACK IRAN – FREE HOSTAGES"

Half the protestors chant, "USA! USA! USA!" Followed by the other half chanting, "Reagan! Reagan! Reagan!"

Owens's hired thugs, white supremacists, and members of the New Nazi Party as protesters and he pays them well. None wear political displays on their clothing because their portrayed political positions are declared through their signs and chants. As directed by Owens, those with Nazi and white supremacists tattoos wear sleeveless jerseys.

Different from the San Diego protest, these hired thugs were purposely not briefed on what is about to happen.

The leader directs the demonstrators in feverish rants against President Jimmy Carter.

Owens continues to watch the scene through binoculars.

When vehicles from the local television station arrive, Owens reaches into the briefcase and retrieves a hand-held radio detonator. He extends the antenna. He places his thumb over the transmit button and continues to watch through the binoculars.

A woman reporter positions the cameraman so that he captures chanting protesters behind her and in the front of the campaign office.

When the reporter is 90 seconds into her report, Owens presses the transmit button. A small fire bomb explodes inside the campaign office. The explosion is powerful enough to disperse ignited fuel throughout the office and blow out the office window. The fire spreads quickly throughout the office interior.

Protesters step back and express horror. A few stumble backward and fall. None of them, except the protest leader, knew the explosion would take place.

The reporter ducks and looks back. The cameraman, who is always ready for the unexpected, zooms in on flames billowing through the office window. He scans the crowd with the camera looking for anyone hurt by the blast. When he sees the Nazi tattoos on some of the protesters' arms, he zooms in on them.

The protest leader flees the scene unnoticed in the chaos.

Ten minutes pass before the protesters regain their composure and some notice the leader is gone. Without a leader, the protesters are uncertain of what to do next. Some call for everyone to board the bus and depart the scene. Others say they must stay because they believe fleeing the scene is a crime.

The reporter begins interviewing protesters. She keeps asking which one of them threw the bomb through the window. Everyone she asks denies knowledge of the bomb.

Some of the protesters board the bus and tell the driver to take them to the drop-off location. The driver informs that he cannot depart without everyone onboard. Some demand loudly to depart. The driver advises he will call his dispatcher on the radio for some guidance.

Fire trucks arrive on the scene and begin fighting the fire.

With the arrival of the fire department, protesters on the bus become fearful of being detained on scene. They jump out of the bus and run off in different directions.

Six of the original protesters remain on scene because their conscience tells them staying is the right thing to do.

Five police cars arrive on scene. The police officers detain all people on the scene.

The TV camera crew is allowed to continue filming and interviewing. All other witnesses are herded against two police cars with three police officers watching over them.

Fifteen minutes later, the firemen have extinguished the fire that had spread to the store next to the campaign office. Four firemen enter the burnt-out campaign office.

Several minutes later, one of the firemen

exits the building and informs the lead fireman that the body of a dead female has been found inside.

At the top of the Sunday evening news, the TV reporter who was at the campaign office when it was destroyed starts with this headline: *RIOTING REAGAN NAZIS FIREBOMB JIMMY CARTER CAMPAIGN OFFICE AND KILL VOLUNTEER CAMPAIGN WORKER.*

The next morning, the firebombing incident fills the programming of all TV network morning shows. Reports of *Rioting Reagan Nazis* firebombing a Jimmy Carter campaign office in Seattle are heard by millions of Americans. All the major newspapers report the incident with the same headline in their evening edition.

On Tuesday morning the Seattle Police hold a press conference to report what they have discovered so far. The press conference is not televised, although reporters from all TV networks and major newspapers are present. The police inform that they have six suspects in custody and have warrants for six more—all protesters. The female victim has been identified as a Carter campaign volunteer who

95

was sleeping on a cot when the explosion occurred. A question and answer period follows.

The reporter from a large city newspaper asks, "Have you identified the *Reagan Nazi* who threw the fire bomb?"

The police captain answers, "So far, we have no evidence that a fire bomb was thrown by anyone. Forensic evidence shows that the bomb was planted prior to the protest and was denoted by radio remote control. We are still investigating."

The revelation about the bomb brings yelps of shock from the reporters. Each of them begin searching their minds for the source that reported a *Reagan Nazi* threw a firebomb through the campaign office window.

Some of the reporters challenge the police captain. He responds, "We have viewed the entire video which includes 90 seconds of the window prior to the explosion. Nothing was thrown through that window during those 90 seconds. All those in custody claim they did not throw the bomb and did not see anyone throw a bomb."

"Captain, can you confirm that the office was destroyed by a fire bomb and the body found was killed by the fire?"

"Yes," the captain responds. "Chemical analysis shows that a fire accelerant was dispersed by an explosive device. And in anticipation of your next question, no, we do not know how the bomb was placed in the office. The coroner is still investigating the death of the volunteer, and the Seattle Police Department is still investigating the entire incident."

After the news conference, TV and newspaper reporters rush back to their offices to review all material and reports on the firebombing incident. Most reporters uncover that the original report from the Seattle TV station claimed a *Reagan Nazi* threw the bomb. But, nothing on the film or in eyewitness accounts substantiate that claim.

Instead of media outlets publicly correcting their news reports, they quietly revise their headline: CARTER CAMPAIGN OFFICE FIREBOMBED AND VOLUNTEER KILLED WHEN REAGAN NAZIS PROTESTED JUST FEET AWAY.

15

San Diego Bay

The California Yacht Club occupies a large area on San Diego Bay, just north of Point Loma. Access to the yacht club docks are gated and manned twenty-four hours a day by armed guards.

The southmost dock is partitioned from the other docks by another security fence and gate with armed guards. The partitioned dock is known as the *Paradisum* dock, named after the 300-foot yacht that berths there. Access to the dock is limited to the crew and selected guests. A ten-space parking lot resides between the security gate and the yacht's gangway.

Bill Owens stops his rent-a-car at the *Paradisum* dock security gate. Owens hands a *Letter of Access* and his Nevada driver's license to the gate guard.

The gate guard checks today's access list. He finds the name William Owens on the list. Today's password for Owens is printed next to his name.

The gate guard hands the access letter and

driver's license back to Owens and asks, "Mr. Owens, what is your password?"

Owens responds with the correct password.

The guard hands Owens a five-inch-by-five-inch card with the number six printed on both sides. "Park in space number six. Leave the card on the dash. The watch at the top of the gangway will know where on the yacht you are supposed to go."

As Owens walks from his car to the gangway, he scans his surroundings. One-half mile to the east, across the bay, navy jets land on a runway at the North Island Naval Air Station. One-mile to the south at Ballast Point, a fast attack submarine departs the submarine base and steams toward the open sea.

The yacht gangway watch wears a nautical style uniform—double breasted dark blue suit with a single gold stripe on each sleeve. A holstered pistol hangs from a wide black-leather belt.

After reading the access letter, the gangway watch unhooks a handset from a bulkhead mounted intercom; he presses a number on the intercom keypad. "Mr. Owens is here to see Mr. Braune."

The gangway watch places the handset on

the hook. "An escort will be here in a few minutes."

Owens nods. He walks clear of the gangway access area and stands by the rail. His eyes watch the activities in San Diego Bay, but his mind recalls how he came to this day on the yacht of one of the world's richest men.

Bill Owens is an alias. He was born and raised as Weston Pyth—son of San Francisco city employees.

Fourteen years ago, Weston Pyth graduated from high school. His appearance and manner at the time were typical for a clean-cut, athletic teenager of the era. He was proud of his three years playing varsity sports and exceptionally proud of his acceptance to the University of California at Berkeley.

His freshman year at Berkeley started in the fall of 1966. His initial major was Engineering. However, he was required to take one elective. He objected to taking courses not related to Engineering. His counselor advised that two electives per year were required to earn a degree—some nonsense about a well-rounded education was U.C. policy. He chose Sociology

100 as his elective for no better reason than he wanted to date a girl taking the same class.

The sociology class changed the direction of his life; not so much the course content as the radical Marxist professor who taught the course. The sociology professor was a charismatic speaker who easily won over many students to his Marxist point of view.

The tenured sociology professor would not allow pro-capitalism or anti-Marxism discussions in this class. Those students who dared to make such comments verbally or in written submissions received lower grades.

Weston was not politically aware. He knew his parents had socialist views but was not certain why. His parents had made a few comments over the years about capitalists victimizing working people, but he did not see anyone victimizing his parents.

As the sociology course progressed, Weston grew angry over the outrageous inequality in America as explained by the professor. According to the professor, capitalism and the U.S. Constitution enabled the strong to victimize the weak. Weston bought it.

When the time came to schedule courses

for his second semester, he enrolled in another sociology course with the same professor and he changed his staff counselor to the sociology professor. Weston adopted a Marxist outlook and became an anti-Americanism activist. His activism took so much of his time that his Engineering courses faded in his priorities and his grades were barely passing.

Under the counsel of the sociology professor, Weston began to question the study of Engineering as his major. "You should abandon this aristocratic pursuit for an Engineering career," the professor advised Weston. "You excel at research and report writing. You should pursue a career in journalism. You would be good at it. You can go to work at a media company and use it as a platform to inform the public on the evils of capitalism. We need to ignite the revolution."

At the end of his second semester, Weston applied to change his major to journalism and his minor to sociology. His application was approved. Journalism and sociology courses were saturated with students and professors who already accepted Marxist ideology. His indoctrination continued.

Weston became an active member in the

Students for a Democratic Society, SDS. As his values changed, so did his appearance. He adopted the hippie image of the time. He grew a full thick beard and his hair grew to shoulder length. His standard apparel became threadbare denim and a red bandana tied around his forehead.

During the closing days of the 1960s while Weston was still an undergraduate, the SDS began to splinter into factions and lost its centrality. Then, the Weather Underground knocked on Weston's door.

The Weather Underground recruiter asked Weston to become a secret operative for the organization. At first, Weston declined. But as the months passed, he became increasingly angry and frustrated with America's involvement in the Vietnam War. At the top of his anger list was the Selective Service that allowed America's rich to avoid the draft and forced America's poor into military service.

As his college graduation day approached, Weston worried more and more about his draft status. He would lose his student deferment when he graduated. Two months before graduation, a Weather Underground recruiter named Jack delivered his recruiting pitch.

Weston was more willing to listen this time.

"What are you plans after graduation?" Jack asked.

"I have accepted a position with *The Long Beach Times*."

"Your activities for the Weather Underground will not interfere with your fulltime job." Jack's tone was sincere.

"I read your charter," Weston told Jack, "I am not a communist, although I do support your cause to destroy American imperialism."

"You are a socialist, right?" Jack asked.

"Yes," Weston affirmed.

"Socialism does not conflict with Weather Underground objectives. Destroying American Imperialism is our primary objective."

Jack asked about Weston's Draft Status, "What is your Draft Lottery Number?"

"Two-eighty-seven, but I currently have a student deferment that I will lose when I graduate."

"Is *The Long Beach Times* concerned about your draft status?"

"No," Weston answered. "They said it is high enough for them to risk hiring me."

"If you join the Weather Underground, we will ensure that you are never drafted into the military."

"How can you do that?!" Weston questioned in an astonished tone.

"We have our sources," Jack confided.

"What do you want me to do?"

"Go to work at *The Long Beach Times*. Portray your life as normal and routine. Occasionally, we will ask you to perform tasks for us."

"Illegal tasks?" Weston had asked with apprehension in his tone.

"Occasionally but not always. I will train you on methods to hide your actions and hide your affiliation with the Weathermen."

Weston responded with silence and a thoughtful expression.

"Are you in for the movement or not?" Jack asked. "If you say no, you will never see me again. If yes, I will brief you on what to expect."

Weston joined the Weather Underground. He graduated from Berkeley, then went to work a week later.

At *The Long Beach Times*, he was assigned to the City Desk Department as junior reporter in the crime section. He was assigned reporting on the petty crimes occurring in the Long Beach, California area.

Reporting the details of petty crimes was boring and unchallenging. His goal as a journalist was to awaken society to the evils of capitalism and the U.S. Constitution. After several months, Weston began writing social commentary into his crime news reports and would speculate without evidence regarding motives. He was warned by his editor to soften his speculation and stick to the facts of an incident.

Occasionally, Jack directed Weston to perform tasks for the Weather Underground. His tasks were mostly transporting individuals from the bus or train station to a foreign registered freighter docked at the Port of Los Angeles. On several occasions, Weston served as a courier of documents or packages.

Three years ago Weston encountered James and Rigney Page when the Pages became victims of labor union violence. James Page owned a small, growing business and his open opposition to labor unions was well known among union activists. When the labor union became violent against the Page family, James and Rigney page showed no fear and lacked no skill in fighting back.

Following his Marxist principles, Weston's

news articles painted the Pages as capitalist victimizers and the labor union as the victim. Through his crime news reports, Weston pushed law enforcement to investigate the Pages for various assaults and bombings against the labor union.

When Weston failed to have James and Rigney Page charged with crimes, he acknowledged to himself that unsubstantiated reporting was not working to serve the Marxist revolution. He became dissatisfied with his contribution to the revolution and asked Jack for assistance in stepping up his actions for the Weathermen.

Jack suggested that Weston go underground. Weston agreed. With Jack's help, Weston faked his own death and became an underground revolutionary and political saboteur.

Jack designed Weston's fake death to look like he had been murdered aboard James Page's cabin cruiser and his body dumped into the ocean. Before disappearing, Weston hid his wristwatch onboard James Page's boat and planted his fingerprints within the boat's interior. But that plot also failed. When police searched the boat several weeks later, no evidence was found that Pyth had ever been aboard.

After he went underground, Weston put off his plan to destroy the Page family and concentrated on performing services for Marxist causes.

Since going underground, he has been hired by radical entities to design and enact plots to destroy politicians who support America's constitutional republic. Money is not important to him; his fees are always cost plus a reasonable living commission.

He is committed to the Marxist revolution. He is confident that the revolution will eventually occur. His confidence is based on the increasing number of Marxists he knows who are infiltrating education systems, judiciary systems, political parties, government service, and the news media.

Weston knows Werner Braune is a powerful capitalist whose reasons for supporting Jimmy Carter are not clear. Weston has dealt with several such capitalists during the past two years. He assumes they bear guilt for being born rich. To overcome their guilt, they commit large amounts of money to support collectivist causes. So, Weston is willing to work with

super wealthy capitalists to achieve his
objective.

"Mr. Owens," a voice calls from behind.

Weston turns and sees a young man in a
steward's white coat, black bow tie, and black
trousers.

The steward says in a subservient manner,
"Mr. Braune is ready for you. Please follow me."

Several minutes later, Bill Owens and
Werner Braune sit at the bar in the *Paradisum's*
main salon. Owens's appearance and manner
is conservative American casual. Braune's
appearance and manner is cultured and
affluent European. They sip coffee and discuss
the effects of Owens's recent sabotage against
Ronald Reagan's campaign.

"You are doing damage," Braune affirms,
"and I want you to expand your operation."

"I'm maxed out," Pyth advises. "I had to
delay an operation because you summoned
me here."

"Yes, I know," Braune acknowledges. "I
want more frequent operations. As you know, I
have people like you conducting operations in
the Midwest and East Coast. I want you to

advise them and monitor their operations. They will report to you instead of me. I have a communications center onboard that you can use as a command center. You may buy additional communications equipment as needed and hire more operatives as needed. You have an open checkbook. I want you to move aboard so that you can report to me daily. I have arranged a stateroom for you."

"Okay," Pyth responds in an agreeable manner. I will start moving aboard tomorrow."

"I want you to move all your records onboard and file them in the communications center. Those records will be safer here than anywhere else."

"Okay. No problem," Pyth responds.

Braune asks, "Was killing that campaign volunteer in Seattle necessary?"

"That was unintentional," Pyth claims. "We did not know she was there. We knocked on the door; no one answered. It was Sunday morning. The office was closed."

Braune expresses thoughtfulness as he concludes, "Her death did make for a better anti-Reagan story."

"Yes it did," Pyth says with confidence.

"I want to see continuous TV reports

discrediting Ronald Reagan. You have talent for creating events that damage Reagan's image, a talent unlike anyone else I have encountered. Teach those field supervisors what you know."

Pyth declares in a tone filled with venom, "I will do my best to stop that fascist from becoming President of the United States."

Braune nods and beams an approving smile.

16

Return of *The Guardians*

Rig sits at his desk in the Curriculum Development Section of the Radioman Schools building. He reviews a lesson plan on the subject of high-frequency receiver operations. The plan already has the approval of the chief and first class petty officers who work for him.

Rig's phone rings. He picks up the handset and recites, "Curriculum Development; this is a non-secure line; Senior Chief Page speaking; how may I help sir or ma'am."

"Hello, Rig. This is Denton Phillips."

Rig quickly visualizes the sandy-haired, always well-dressed, ex air force intelligence officer. Denton had recruited Rig into *The Guardians* three years ago.

"Hello, Denton, a pleasure hearing from you again."

"We need your assistance. Can you meet with me this evening?"

"You're in San Diego?"

"Yes," Denton confirms.

"Okay. Where?"

"Holiday Inn on Rosecrans."

"What time?"

"Twenty-one-thirty. Room 209. Wear civvies."

"I'll be there!" Rig says with enthusiasm.

Denton hangs up.

Rig glances at his watch. He is a few minutes late for his daily lunchtime exercise routine at the base gym. He grabs his cover; then walks quickly out the door.

On his way to the gym, Rig reflects on the secret organization he joined three years ago. *The Guardians* was originally formed in the 1870s to fight against Southern States that refused to comply with the U.S. Constitution and federal civil rights laws.

During its 110 years in existence, *The Guardians* have focused on exposing and destroying those in power who engage in unconstitutional activities that result in harming innocent people. *The Guardians* restricts its operations to the United States, although it has resources overseas that provides intelligence and logistic services. The organization is well funded, but by whom or what is only known at the highest levels of the secret organization.

Shortly after Rig was recruited into *The Guardians*, Denton Phillips offered Rig resources and weapons to fight a lawless and revengeful labor union that threatened his family. During his tour in Spain, he used *Guardian* resources to defeat a Spanish crime family that was involved in espionage against the United States.

Because *The Guardians* provide protection for his family, Rig has committed lifelong loyalty to the secret organization. Whatever Denton wants from him this time, Rig is committed to provide it with one-hundred percent effort.

17

Marriott Hotel
Berkeley, California

Weston Pyth responds to the knock and opens the door to his hotel room. As expected and on time, Jack stands in the hallway and smiles at Pyth.

The appearance of both men has changed over the years. They have discarded their 1960s hippie appearance for a more conservative look. A look that is necessary to deceive an unaware and unworldly public. Today, both of them wear summer suits and are neatly groomed.

Pyth invites Jack in. The two men shake hands and exchange sincere greetings.

Pyth does not know Jack's last name. He is not certain that Jack is actually his real name.

Jack approached Pyth eleven years ago during Pyth's last semester at U.C. Berkeley. Jack had convinced Pyth to perform services for the Weather Underground. Pyth did not become an active member; he only provided services for the Weather Underground at

115

Jack's request. Jack is Pyth's sole contact with the Weather Underground.

When Pyth decided to go underground, Jack assisted him with identification, a fake passport, and guidance on how to live underground. Six months ago when Pyth told Jack that he was hired by Werner Braune to sabotage the Reagan campaign, Jack enlisted Pyth to spy on Braune and provide reports on Braune's political and business activities.

They sit down at a table near a window that provides a spectacular view of the San Francisco Bay. A bottle of wine stands on the table next to a tray of light snacks.

Jack picks up the bottle of wine and reads the label. "You remembered my favorite. I am appreciative."

Pyth pours wine into two glasses and passes a glass to Jack.

"To the revolution," they toast, clinking their glasses.

Jack queries, "How is your infiltration into Werner Braune's empire?"

"At his request, I recently moved aboard his yacht. He wants daily briefings. I am discovering more about him and his business and political associations."

Jack is impressed with Pyth's infiltration. He says, "I have been reading all the bad press about Reagan in the newspapers and news magazines. Mostly unsubstantiated, I must add. Is that your work?"

"A lot of it is my work," Pyth answers. "Braune recently put all his political operatives under my control. So the effort will be better coordinated now."

"Looks like you have gained his trust," Jack assesses. "I assume you called this meeting because you have more information about him."

"Yes." Pyth hands Jack a large manila envelope. "More on his business interests."

Jack opens the envelope and begins reading the fifteen handwritten sheets of paper. His concentration increases with each page. Obviously, the information is revealing. Every couple of sheets, he sips wine.

After reading the last sheet, Jack asks, "Where did you get this information?"

"I have access to the radio room aboard his yacht. He has a sophisticated, encrypted-teletype connection to his Geneva office."

Jack asks, "Can you get me a copy of the frequency list for that teletype connection and

117

a copy of the encryption codes?"

"Yes on the frequencies. The list is taped to the radio equipment. I'm not sure about the encryption codes. They are inventoried every day. I'll let you know on the codes."

"Excellent," Jack responds. Then, he asks, "What do you know about *The Trajan Consortium*?"

"Never heard of it," Pyth answers.

"I need you to be on the alert. If you gain any information regarding Braune and that consortium, I want to know about it immediately."

Pyth asks, "Call the same number and leave a recorded message, then?"

"Yes," Jack confirms. "I check for messages several times per day."

The two men are silent while they finish drinking their glass of wine.

Jack stands, "I need to go."

Pyth pours more wine into Jack's glass. Indicating he wants Jack to stay for three more sips.

"Something on your mind?" Jack asks.

Pyth responds, "Yes. I often wonder how much my actions affect the success of Weathermen operations. I went underground because I wanted to contribute more to the revolution. Rarely do I see news reports of sabotage that are typically Weathermen methods. Is the objective the same? Are we a deterrent to American imperialism?"

Jack assures, "I can tell you without doubt that our organization is strong and growing. I know it is difficult for you to see our successes without knowing what operations the Weathermen are involved. Our cell organization does not allow notifications down and across the structure. The cell structure is essential to keeping us strong because no one person can betray the entire organization. Because we are a cell structure, I only have one contact who is my supervisor in the organization. He assures me that our cell contributes significantly to Weathermen's success. So, I ask you to continue your best effort to destroy rich and powerful fascists like Werner Braune and Ronald Reagan."

Pyth nods, indicating he is satisfied with Jack's answer.

Jack downs the last gulp of wine in his glass. "Now, I must go," he insists.

Outside the Marriot, Jack enters a taxi and tells the driver to take him to the train station. Jack sits sideways in the back seat and occasionally looks out the back window to see if he is being followed. His skill and experience tell him that he is not being followed. As they approach the train station, Jack instructs the driver to the side entrance.

When the driver stops at the train station side entrance, he pays the driver with an exact fifteen percent tip. Jack never over-tips or under-tips so that he is less memorable to the driver should the driver ever be questioned about his passenger trips.

Jack enters the train station; then goes directly to the main entrance where he exits the station and enters another taxi. He gives the taxi driver the address of a rent-by-the-month parking garage. During the ride to the parking garage, Jack sits sideways in the back seat and occasionally looks out the back window.

The single, gated, vehicle entrance-exit to the parking garage faces a one-way, narrow street. If there is a vehicle tailing the taxi, the one-way, narrow street is where Jack will easily identify the tail. He is confident he is not being followed.

The taxi drops Jack at the vehicle entrance-exit. He takes the elevator to the third floor where he has a Volkswagen bus camper parked. He unlocks the door and steps in.

All the window curtains are drawn, allowing him complete privacy. He changes his clothes and puts on a simple disguise—a long hair wig, fake glasses, and a hat.

After locking the Volkswagen, he walks down the back stairs to the ground floor where there is a walk-in-and-out entrance that is on the opposite side of the garage from the vehicle entrance-exit.

A three-year-old, four-door sedan with driver waits for him at the curb. He sits down in the backseat; then tells the driver, "Consulate." The heavily tinted windows of the sedan make it nearly impossible to see the passenger from the outside.

When the sedan is one block away from the Soviet Consulate, Jack removes his disguise wig, glasses, and hat. The sedan stops at the gate to the consulate employee's parking lot. The driver lowers the front and back power windows. The gate guard looks inside the vehicle, recognizes the driver and the passenger, and allows the vehicle to pass. The driver parks the sedan in the underground parking garage.

Jack goes to his office in the Operations Center where he stows his disguise and changes into his normal office attire. Then, he proceeds to his KGB supervisor's office and gives a briefing on the information passed to him by Weston Pyth.

18

Sacramento, California

Weston Pyth, alias Bill Owens, enters a restaurant two blocks away from the governor's mansion. He goes directly to the hostess at the podium. "I am having lunch with Mr. Mark Ringard. I believe he has a reservation in his name."

The hostess glances down at the reservation list. "Are you Mr. Owens?"

"Yes. I have never met John Ringard. Please point out his table."

"He is out on the patio. Please follow me."

As they walk through the main floor of the restaurant, Pyth notes the quality furniture, table linens, and white-coat waiters. Diners are well dressed and well groomed. Obviously, this is where the rich and affluent eat lunch. Pyth wears a tailor-made three-piece suit. His appearance fits the environment. Those who glance at him accept his presence as legitimate.

As Pyth approaches Ringard's table, he notices that the closest diners to Ringard's table are twenty-feet away, allowing his conversation with Ringard to be private.

Ringard stands and offers his hand. Pyth takes it.

"A pleasure to meet you, Mr. Owens," Ringard states with a cautious smile.

"My pleasure," Pyth responds.

The waiter asks for their order. Both order the soup of the day, half sandwich, and iced tea.

Ringard inquires, "Mr. Owens, I have known Bob Latori since 1966. When he set up this meeting, he said you and he have been friends for a long time. He never mentioned your name before he arranged this meeting. I am curious as to how you and Bob are associated."

"We worked on the same political action committees," Pyth informs. "Bob told me that you two were stationed in Saigon together."

"That's right," Ringard affirms. "During the years after the army, Bob and I also worked on political action committees together. That was before I became a California State employee."

The waiter delivers their lunch.

For the next few minutes, they pause their conversation while they take several mouthfuls of their lunch.

Ringard says, "Bob said that you wanted to discuss the November election. I must mention that as a California State employee, I cannot involve myself in politics."

Pyth inquires, "Your office receives the approved version of voting ballots for reproduction and distribution, correct?"

Ringard replies with concern in both his expression and tone. "Yes. That's correct."

Pyth informs, "Bob said you would cooperate in providing me with the final version of the ballot form and a copy of the associated punch card."

Ringard's body becomes stiff as he expresses astonishment. Then, defiance takes over his manner.

Before Ringard can object, Pyth says, "Bob told me you and he had colluded in the past to cheat on elections. Bob said you would be cooperative this time, also. I lead an organization whose objective is to ensure that President Carter gets the most votes in the November election."

"That's unnecessary," Ringard protests. "News reports show that Carter will win in landslide. Carter has a constant ten-point lead in the polls."

"Don't believe the polls," Pyth declares in a knowing tone.

"Bob is being reckless," Ringard states in a concerned tone. "Expanding our scope increases danger of discovery."

Pyth asks in a warning tone, "Do you want me to tell Bob that you're not cooperating?"

"I'll play," Ringard concedes. "How do I deliver copies to you?"

"Bob will contact you and arrange another meeting. Not with me but one of my associates."

Ringard stands, tosses his napkin onto the table, turns, and walks away shaking his head.

As Ringard walks away, Pyth concludes that too many political activists are becoming lazy because of the wide spread in approval polls between Reagan and Carter. He decides to order some more polls to be conducted. But this time, the polls will be designed to show the spread is narrowing; then, like before, have Betsy and her peers in the media publish them.

A narrowing spread will get them desperate and off their asses, Pyth concludes.

19

The Holiday Inn on Rosecrans
San Diego, California

Rig enters Denton's hotel room. The two men shake hands and exchange enthusiastic greetings. Denton wastes no time getting down to business.

Denton asks, "Have you heard of an organization called *The Trajan Consortium*?"

"Yes," Rig answers. "They're some sort of secret society, right?"

"How do you know about them?" Denton asks.

"I heard the name mentioned a couple of times when I was in Europe. I do not remember who mentioned it. That's all I remember."

Denton expresses disappointment as he says, "You've spent so much time undercover in Europe; I thought, maybe, you crossed their path."

"Not to my knowledge," Rig states with certainty. "Who are they?"

"We know very little. We believe they are rich Europeans who are funding political sabotage in America. We were tracking a money transfer that we believed originated with *The Trajans* and discovered the receiving bank account is owned by an American named William Owens. When Mr. Owens arrived at the bank to pick up cash, I had operatives there to tail him. Imagine our surprise when we discovered that William Owens was an alias for one Mr. Weston Pyth, formerly of Long Beach California and who is presumed dead by the general public."

Ring flinches and expresses surprise.

"We began tailing Pyth and discovered he was engaged in political sabotage against Ronald Reagan. We infiltrated several of Pyth's sabotage operations, hoping he would lead us to *The Trajan Consortium*."

"What do you mean by political sabotage?" Rig asks.

"Did you read or watch TV news about so-called *Reagan Fascists* killing a Carter campaign volunteer in Seattle while protesting in front of a Carter campaign office?"

"Yes," Rig responds. "The volunteer was killed when a protestor threw a firebomb through the window."

"Do you believe what was reported?"

Rig expresses surprise at the question and responds, "Shouldn't I?"

"Two days after the incident, the Seattle Police Department held an untelevised news conference. They told the media that the bomb was not thrown but planted in the office by unknown persons. Also, the police revealed that the six so-called protesters who were arrested at the scene were paid to demonstrate and only three of them are registered to vote. None of the witnesses at the scene saw anyone throw a bomb. The paid protesters were released without charge."

"I don't remember seeing any of that in the news," Rig states.

"That's because reporters covered it up. Apparently, some reporters are not above misrepresenting these events."

Rig asks, "How do you know what really happened, then?"

"The truth was reported in several financial newsletters," Denton answers.

"So, they hate Ronald Reagan so much that they must deceive the public?"

"That's our view and *The Trajan Consortium* is funding it."

Rig takes on a serious expression while

129

asking, "I assume that law enforcement is investigating these acts of terrorism."

"The police and FBI are aware of the crimes and they are investigating. They have not yet discovered that *The Trajan Consortium* is responsible or even that it exists.

"Because innocent Americans are being harmed and killed and being denied their constitutional rights, *The Guardians Council* has directed we expose *The Trajan Consortium* and destroy Pyth's operation. When we have enough evidence, we will turn it over to the FBI."

After a short pause, Rig asks, "So, where do I fit it to this situation?"

"You remember Weston Pyth, right?" Denton asks.

"Yes. He was that reporter for *The Long Beach Times* who spread lies about me and my family. My father told me Pyth went missing several years ago."

"Actually, Pyth assumed a new identity and went underground," Denton informs. "Looks like political sabotage is his career now. After Pyth's Seattle operation, we lost track of him. We need to find him again and interrogate him this time."

"And you think I can help in some way?"

Denton explains, "Several years ago, Pyth was on a campaign to destroy you and your family. If you have any knowledge that might lead us to him or cause him to come after you, we could pick up his trail when he surfaces."

Rig explains, "Pyth tried to frame his disappearance as being killed by my father."

Denton's eyes go wide with hopeful surprise. "Do you have any evidence that Pyth did that?"

"No. I threw the evidence into the ocean."

"Tell me what happened from beginning to end."

Rig explains, "Just before I departed for Spain two-years ago, I went on a fishing trip with my father and my uncle. We went to Catalina on my father's boat. One evening I found Pyth's wristwatch in a storage void on the boat.

"I knew Pyth had disappeared. When I found Pyth's watch onboard, I thought my father had killed Pyth and thrown his body overboard. But months later when I was in Spain, events caused me to change my mind and believe that Pyth attempted to frame my father by planting his watch on my father's boat."

"What changed your mind?" Denton asks.

"The Long Beach Police and FBI showed up at my father's boat with a warrant to search for evidence that Weston Pyth had been onboard. My father told me Pyth had never been onboard.

"Now that I know Pyth went underground and took on a new identity, I am confident that he planted his watch onboard and planted evidence somewhere to lead the police to my father's boat. Obviously, Pyth knows nothing about boat maintenance. If he had known, he would not have designed such a poor plan."

Denton queries, "What about boat maintenance that foiled Pyth's plan?"

"Well maintained boats are periodically scrubbed down with freshwater inside and out; thereby washing away fingerprints and increasing the chance of someone finding objects not properly stowed."

Denton considers Rig's explanation; then, he asks, "Anything else on Pyth since your father's boat was searched?"

"My father says nothing has happened since his boat was searched, and I had heard nothing about Pyth until you informed me about him a few minutes ago."

Denton asks, "Did you tell anyone about the watch and what you did with it?"

"I never told anyone about it, till now."

"Was there anything about the watch that only someone who saw it would know?"

"It was a gold plated watch with a flexible band. On the back was an inscription from Pyth's parents congratulating him on his graduating from college."

Denton expresses a conspiring smile and says, "I think we have something to bring Pyth to the surface."

Rig raises his eyebrows and expresses curiosity.

Denton explains, "If he thinks you have his watch, he might surface to confirm it before he anonymously notifies authorities. If he gets close to you, my operatives will detect him. Are you willing to be the bait?"

"Sure," Rig responds willingly. "But how do we make Pyth believe that I have his watch?"

"I will take care of that," Denton states confidently. "Can you meet me here again in three days—same time?"

"I will be here," Rig promises.

20

Phoenix, Arizona

Cameron Luce walks out of the elevator on the tenth floor and searches for room 1005. The tenth floor of the Poplar Building contains rent-by-the-day offices and clerical services. He is on the way to a meeting as ordered by his boss, the VP of Engineering and Development at ACP Corporation. Cameron was told to meet with Mr. Owens who would ask technical questions about the company's products. Cameron was ordered to answer all of Mr. Owens's questions and comply with all of Mr. Owens's requests.

Cameron Luce opens the door to room 1005. A man in an expensive gray suit who appears to be in his mid-thirties sits at a small conference table. A tray of coffee with croissant sandwiches and Danish pastries sit in the center of the table.

Weston Pyth looks up and sees exactly what he expects see. Luce is a thin man of medium height. His blond hair hangs slightly over his ears, and his mustache and beard are trimmed short. He wears a white long-sleeve shirt and tie with summer weight gray slacks. The temperature is too hot today for Cameron to wear his gray suit jacket.

"Mr. Owens?" Luce inquires.

"Yes." Weston Pyth answers. "Please take a seat." He points to the tray and offers, "What would you like?"

"Just some coffee, please."

Pyth pours two cups of coffee.

As he pushes a cup of coffee and a half & half mini-cup toward Luce, Pyth asks, "You are the manager of programming for the ACP vote counting machines, correct?"

"Yes," Luce responds.

"In layman terms, explain how a machine counts votes."

Luce explains, "In the voting booth, the names of candidates on the ballot are aligned with a punch card, similar to an IBM computer card. The voter punches a hole in the card next to the candidates name. When the voter is done punching holes for his choices, the voter drops the card into a box.

"After the polls close, the punched cards are run through an ACP vote counting machine. Each candidate has position on the punch oard. For example, the second name in the candidate list for president is aligned with column A row 2 or as we call it, A2. The ACP program connects position A2 with the candidate's name and adds a vote to that candidate.

"It's basically the same for paper ballots where the voter fills in a circle or block next to the candidates name. The circles or blocks are read by position, like the card."

Luce sips his coffee, then reaches for a Danish.

Pyth asks, "How many states use ACP voting equipment for vote counting?"

"Twenty-three."

"What if there are two holes punched for president?" Pyth asks.

"The computer rejects the card and no vote for president is counted by the computer."

Pyth nods, expressing he understand. "How do you fix an error in the program?"

"That rarely happens. We run the program through vigorous testing before installing it in our voting machines. We had only two bugs that got into the field and they were minor printing format errors."

"How is the program installed in the voting

machines?" Pyth inquires.

"In our lab at ACP, we have devices that download the vote counting program into programmable microchips. The microchip is then plugged into the CPU motherboard. When the counting machine is powered up, our program starts running.

"When we need to make program changes for the next election, we download the revised program into microchips and distribute the microchips to our field service technicians. Our field service technicians go to the government buildings where our computers are located and swap the microchips."

"What about the program for the November elections? Is it finished? Is it installed?"

"Oh, no," Luce responds. "That's months away. We usually distribute the programmed microchips about two weeks before the election."

"Can you, personally, make changes to the code that no one else knows about?"

"Yes. I am the one who approves the program and compiles the code. Compilation is the last step before loading the microchips."

"What about security?" Pyth asks. "Who safeguards the programs and compilations?

Who can see the final version of the program?"

"Only me," Luce answers. "It's all password protected. The final source code can only be accessed by me."

"I see," Pyth declares with a tone of finality. "I want you to make modifications in the program that changes twelve percent of the votes for Reagan to votes for Carter."

"I can't do that. It's illegal," Luce protests. "I would be fired. No other computer company would hire me after that."

"You will not be fired or discovered," Pyth assures. "I represent the people who control your employment. Do what I say and you will keep your job."

"But it's so illegal and morally wrong?" Luce protests.

Pyth challenges, "Do you not see the justice in keeping the federal government safe from racists and fascists?"

Luce becomes conflicted between what he knows to be illegal and his political principles. But he still expresses defiance against what he has been told to do.

"Cheating on the vote count is not necessary," Luce asserts. "The polls say Carter is ahead nationwide by ten percent. Every day on the news, they report Reagan doesn't have a chance."

"Wake up, Cameron. The polls and the news are controlled by people like me."

Luce flinches and blinks his eyes and expresses surprise at Mr. Owens's words. Then, he expresses doubt.

Pyth sees that Luce needs more motivation.

"Mr. Luce, when you applied for employment with ACP seven years ago, you stated that you were never in the military." Pyth opens the folder, pulls out a sheet of paper, and pushes the paper to Luce.

Anxiety overcomes Luce's manner as he stares down at a copy of his DD Form 214, his record of military service. His face turns red and he begins to perspire.

"I have other documents from your two years in the army," Pyth reveals. "The documents show that you were discharged from the army after you were caught engaging in homosexual acts with other soldiers. According to the records of the Article 15 hearing, you were caught in the barracks duty room giving blow jobs to some barracks residents."

Luce's heart pounds in his chest.

Pyth continues. "During the two weeks prior to this meeting, those I represent—those who own ACP— had private detectives following you. Those detectives report that you frequent The Golden Barn Lounge, a gay bar here in the Phoenix. Obviously, giving blow jobs is one of your favorite pastimes. The detectives report that most nights at The Golden Barn you go out into the parking as much as five times and give blow jobs to a different guy each time."

Pyth retrieves three enlarged photographs from the file folder and pushes them toward Luce.

Luce expresses defeat as he stares at the photographs that must have been taken with a night-vision telescopic-lens camera. Each photograph shows him in the backseat of a car with his mouth wrapped around an erect penis.

Pyth promises, "You do what I say and tell no one about this and you keep your job. And your family and coworkers do not find out about your cock-sucking fetish. I am told you are a top notch programmer and excellent manager. The owners of ACP do not want to fire you, but they have priorities."

"Okay," Luce agrees while nodding his head. "I will do it."

In an authoritative tone, Pyth orders, "You will send me a copy of the altered source code before you compile it. I will notify you later on how to contact me."

"I need to know something," Luce says in a pleading tone.

"What?"

"Does anyone at my company know about what you have told me to do? My VP sent me here."

"No one except the owners of ACP and me," Pyth states sincerely. "Your VP does not know and he will not ask you questions about this meeting."

"Owners?" Luce questions.

"The path to the owners of ACP is complex; don't waste your time trying to discover who they are."

21

The Holiday Inn on Rosecrans
San Diego, California

Rig enters Denton's hotel room. He sees a tall and muscular black man standing across the room. Rig recognizes him but cannot remember from where.

Denton performs introductions. "Rigney Page this is Larry Franklin."

Rig and Larry shake hands. Rigs says, "I have seen you before, but I can't—"

Larry reminds Rig, "Panama—three years ago. I was part of the squad that raided Mendoza's hacienda. I was the one who coldcocked that navy officer who had you pinned to the floor."

Rig exhibits an embarrassing grin and comments, "Now I remember. I never thanked you for the assistance. So, thank you."

Larry expresses an understanding smile and nods.

Denton tells Rig, "We have come up with a plan to entice Pyth to come after you."

Rig looks Denton in the eyes and expresses

interest.

"We believe Pyth has your father under surveillance. Not all the time, but randomly about twelve hours per week. A van jammed with surveillance equipment parks near your family home in Seal Beach and near your father's business in Long Beach. The van is owned by a two-man private detective agency. The two partners are also the technician who operate the van.

"We put tails on those private detectives. One afternoon during a lunch break, a hippy-looking gentleman in a cheap leisure suit sat down at their table. They exchanged some words; then one of the private detectives gave leisure suit some recording tapes and video tapes. Leisure suit handed one of the private detectives an envelope containing money.

"We put a tail on the leisure suit, and we discovered that he and Weston Pyth were fraternity brothers in college. Leisure suit is also an active member of what little remains of that secret commie organization, *The Longjumeau Alliance*.

"Our plan is to have those private detectives record you telling the story of finding Weston Pyth's wristwatch on your father's boat."

"Do my parents know about the surveillance?"

"Yes," Denton affirms. "We told them several months ago. We believe that is when the surveillance started."

"You talked with my parents?"

"We communicate with your parents through Brian Sanderhill."

Rig conveys understanding as he remembers the lawyer, Brian Sanderhill, who *The Guardians* provided to represent Rig and his father during the Mad Bomber Case several years back. Because of Rig's commitment and service to *The Guardians*, Denton promised that *The Guardians* would protect his family from further violence and intimidation by the CLWUA labor union and by any remnants of *The Longjumeau Alliance*. Denton also promised that Brian Sanderhill would provide legal assistance should they be threatened again.

Rig asks, "How did they respond to being surveilled?"

"They said they already suspected it."

"That must be really disrupting my parent's lives." Rig expresses concern for his parents .

"They were not concerned after Brian told

them that the surveillance averages twelve hours per week. Brian advised them to act as if they did not know about the surveillance because he is collecting evidence against those who hired the detectives."

Rig appears perplexed as asks, "Twelve hours a week doesn't make sense. What kind of surveillance are they conducting?"

"Mostly video recording and some conversation recording. For the conversations, they are using audio sensitive equipment with handheld parabolic microphones."

Rig asks, "Are there hidden microphones in my parents' home and my Dad's business?"

"No," Denton responds. "Part of the protection service we provide to your parents is monthly sweeps for surveillance equipment."

Rig appears thoughtful for a few moments; then he inquires, "You said the surveillance started about two months ago. Do you know why?"

"We don't know for certain. The surveillance started just about the same time your orders were issued transferring you stateside."

Rig expresses surprise as he concludes, "So they're after me."

"That is what we believe," Denton

acknowledges.

Rig asks, "Do you have any idea as to what they want?"

"Pyth wants to destroy you and your family. He is a Marxist and you and your family are the epitome the capitalist American Dream. You blew up his car and he failed at framing your father for murder. I think it is personal with him. I think you can draw him out into the open."

"How?"

"When they are listening, you will hint that you have Pyth's watch. Pyth will want the authorities to catch you with that watch. So, he will attempt to verify your possession of the watch before he contacts the authorities. He can't risk someone taking the watch away from you; he will need to get close to you to verify the watch is his. We expect him to search your apartment and your parents' home. We will have him in our sights, then."

Rig conveys understanding. He glances over at Larry Franklin. His expression asks what's Larry's part in this plot to bring out Weston Pyth.

Denton explains, "Franklin and his team will have your back—bodyguards. Protection in case Pyth acts unpredictably."

Rig raises an eyebrow in an inquisitive expression. "Unpredictably?"

"Yes. If he decides not to notify the authorities and acts violently toward you."

"You mean Pyth might decide to just kill me and my father and be done with it."

"That's right," Denon affirms.

Rig responds in a defiant tone. "Understand this, Denton. I will offer up my safety as bait, but I don't want that commie son-of-bitch getting anywhere close to my family. I am willingly acting as bait so that *The Guardians* can permanently remove Pyth from being a danger to my family. If you can't assure my family's safety, then I will not act as bait."

"We will protect you and your family," Denton responds in a caring and sincere manner. "Pyth has a cause to serve. Just killing you would not serve his cause. I think that Pyth acting unpredictably is very low risk. Will you trust me on this?"

Rig calms his tone and responds, "Yes, of course. I trust you with my life."

"And I trust you with mine," Denton responds honestly.

22

The Watergate Hotel
Washington D.C.

Well known among the international affluent is that when you want to discuss business with Werner Braune, you must travel to him. However, when U.S. Senators want to discuss business with Braune, Braune travels to them.

On this day, Braune travels by taxi to The Watergate Hotel with only one bodyguard. Both Braune and his bodyguard wear sunglasses and are dressed in mid-priced golfing attire. They do not draw attention.

Braune has an appointment with Senator Comings who is the chair and vice-chair of committees whose legislation affect Braune's businesses. The appointment location, a spacious suite on an upper floor, was negotiated between Braune's chief aid and the senator's chief-of-staff. The reservation for the room is in the name of a low-level member of the senator's staff and reserved with the staff-member's personal American Express Card. All protocols for a secret meeting between

Braune and the senator have been executed.

Braune and Senator Comings sit alone in the living room area of the large suite. Braune's bodyguard and the senator's aid wait in the hallway.

Braune opens his briefcase and removes a metal device the size of a cigar box and places it on the coffee table that is positioned between the two men. He flips a switch on top of the box.

The senator casts a questioning glance at Braune.

"To defeat any listening or recording devices," Braune explains.

The senator nods understanding; he had agreed to the device during pre-meeting discussions. Senator Comings has his own dampening device hidden in the room; Braune had agreed to that.

Senator Comings opens the conversation. "Your lobbyists made a promise that I want to hear directly from you. My understanding is that If my *Clean Air* bill is passed into law with the restrictions on U.S. oil production that your lobbyists specified, you will prevent Ronald Reagan from becoming president."

"That is correct," Braune affirms, "I also promised that your supporting PACs will rcooive millions in donations. However, the *Clean Air* bill must pass into law beforo September fifteenth in order to hold me to both promises."

"May I ask why that date?" the senator inquires.

"Because I will need time before the November elections to implement my plan to destroy Reagan."

"You are already doing that, right?" the senator challenges. "I read the newspapers and watch the nightly news."

"Yes. Those anti-Reagan incidents are my doing, and I have more destructive actions planned. If your bill passes with the oil production decreases I specified, more influence and more money will rally against Reagan. I have the power to capture that increased influence and money and use it effectively against Reagan."

Senator Comings stares at Braune in an attempt to find sincerity in those promises. Braune has made good on his promises in the past.

Senator Comings advises, "My clean air bill already decreases U.S. oil production by fifteen percent. It will become law with that percentage because I have the votes for fifteen percent. You are asking for twenty percent which does not have enough support in congress to pass into law."

Publicly, the senator claims that a clean American environment is his motivation for reduced oil production in America. He accuses anyone who criticizes his legislation as being *pollution for profit advocates*.

Scientists have reported that the production restrictions specified in the bill will not improve the environment because the bill does not reduce consumption. The senator publicly accuses those scientists as being *puppets of big oil*.

Senator Comings's real motivation for the restrictions on American oil production is his global-socialist ideology. He believes that America does not deserve its prosperity and influence in the world and should subordinate itself to the benefit of other nations. As a globalist, he supports redistribution of American wealth to less-rich nations. The senator believes that America has benefited enough through its exploitation of other countries and now is payback time.

The senator knows this agreement with

Braune reeks of corruption and anti-Americanism and benefits foreigners over Americans. He believes that damaging America's economy and prosperity makes America ripe for establishment of a socialist society.

"How will you prevent Reagan from being elected president?" the senator asks.

"I prefer to keep my secrets," Braune responds.

The senator expresses thoughtfulness. Then he reveals, "I am short twenty-two votes for my bill with your desired percentage, mostly by members from oil-producing states. I am thinking that if you have the power and influence to prevent Reagan from becoming president, then you have the power and influence to persuade those opposing twenty-two votes to change their vote. Without their vote, the bill will never be delivered to President Carter's desk to be signed into law."

Braune expresses understanding and offers, "Give their names. I will have my lobbyists work on flipping them."

23

The Page Residence
Seal Beach, California

The Page family home on Seal Way faces the fence of the Naval Weapons Station. A twenty-foot-wide concrete walkway separates the front of the Page home from the chain link fence of the Naval Station. The beach is a short walk southward on the concrete walkway.

The Page home is a small three-story structure. The exterior is stucco. A small courtyard outside the front door separates the house from the concrete walkway that leads to the beach.

Even with the attic family room, the house is only eighteen-hundred square feet. The interior of the house contains a mismatch of furniture styles that Rigney's parents purchased at auctions and yard sales. All the floors are polished hardwood. Area rugs of different colors cover most of the hardwood floors.

On this Friday evening, the Page family sits around the dining room table. They eat tacos in celebration of their traditional Friday night taco dinners from decades ago. James Page, Rig's father, sits at one end of the table and Margaret Page, Rig's mother, sits at the other end. Rig and his sister, Terri, sit on one side of the table. Rig's sister, Kate, and her five-year-old daughter sit on the other side of the table.

Missing from the family gathering is Kate's husband, Bradley, who has been banned from the Page family home and from all Page business locations. During a political discussion in the Page home two years ago, Bradley called James Page a fascist and a racist. James Page banned Bradley from the Page Home and business locations for life plus 50 years. Bradley works as an Orange County social worker and is a boisterous anti-capitalism activist.

Each of the Page family members take their turn in updating the family about their lives.

Rig's youngest sister, Terri, tells of her new actress role in a daily TV soap opera. She recently moved to Glendale to be closer to the TV studio. She is still single, and there is no special man in her life.

Rig's sister, Kate, the second oldest of the Page children, advises she was recently promoted to principal of a middle school in

Santa Ana.

Rig's mother reports that she is still the manager of the private personnel agency where she has worked for the past twenty-five years. She complains that the recession has slowed business to a crawl.

James Page sadly reports that he had to lay off six of his employees and sell his cabin cruiser because of the recession. He expresses hope that Ronald Reagan beats President Carter in the upcoming election. "Reagan has promised to end the recession through tax cuts and reduced business regulations. Whereas President Carter promises continued shared misery through increased redistribution of wealth, high taxes, and increased government regulations."

Rig challenges his father, "Did Carter actually say that he promises continued *'shared misery'* if he is reelected."

"Not his exact words," James Page admits. "But that is what we will get if he is allowed to continue his policies into a second term."

"You always misrepresent President Carter's actions," Kate Page accuses. "Why do you do that?"

"I do not misrepresent Carter's actions,"

James Page asserts. "I correctly predict the consequences of his actions on the country."

Terri Page remains silent with a concerned expression on her face. She worries about another family quarrel over politics between her father and her sister.

In an authoritarian tone, Rig's mother reminds everyone, "We all promised no politics this weekend."

The others nod in agreement, and they all fall silent.

Terri breaks the silence. She looks at Rig and says, "Tell us about what you did for fun in Spain and Italy."

Rig spends the next 30 minutes detailing his adventures of sailing and scuba diving off the shores of Spain and Italy and of the Spanish and Italian friends he made. He states that his navy duties were *just routine*. He did not tell them about Bella.

After Rig's mother and sisters go to bed, Rig and his father sit on the dimly lit back porch of the family home. They sip Irish whiskey and discuss the FBI search of James's boat several years before.

Sixty feet away across the back yard on the other side of the single-car garage in the alley known as Seal Way, private detectives use acoustic surveillance to listen and record the Page's conversation.

James Page recalls, "The warrant said personal items of Weston Pyth, but he was never on my boat. I have no idea why they thought they would find anything belonging to that son-of-bitch on my boat."

Rig explains, "Warrant to search means they had evidence to convince a judge that something belonging to Pyth was on the boat."

"Pyth was never on my boat," James declares.

Rig speculates, "Pyth could have planted a personal item on the boat when you or Uncle Dave were not onboard."

"Only cleaning crews had access to the boat when I was not there. They're bonded."

"It's still possible that Pyth or someone who specializes in unauthorized entry went aboard and planted evidence."

"Like what?" James becomes curious.

"Something that can easily be connected to him, like, maybe, an inscribed class ring or wristwatch or maybe some kind of I.D. card."

"But the police did not find anything," James insists.

"If it was something valuable, like a ring or wristwatch, maybe an employee of the cleaning company found it and kept it."

"The police went over the entire boat with a fine tooth comb," James asserts. "They even removed the cases of beer from the forward void and spent an hour searching in there."

"I remember the forward void," Rig says in a tone of fond remembrance "It was one of my assigned cleaning spaces when I was a boy. Even after I joined the navy, you had me cleaning that void and had me stowing beer there. I remember you insisted I clean that void just before that fishing trip to Catalina, just before I went to Spain."

"I remember," James says fondly. "After you and the girls left the nest, I had to hire a boat cleaning company to keep the boat ship-shape. I never had a problem with theft from those cleaners."

After a few moments of silence, James Page sighs and expresses satisfaction as he says, "I am glad it is all over, now . . . that mad-bomber thing and Pyth gone. The world is a better place without Pyth in it."

"I want to take you and Mom to dinner tomorrow night," Rig offers. "I have made reservations at *Lombardi's*."

"Sounds good, Rig. Your mother needs a night out. I'll let her know."

Rig stands and says, "Been a long day for me. I'm going to bed."

"Are you settled in?" James asks. "Do you have everything you need?"

"Yes. I put the rollaway bed in the family room and I brought a small suitcase with everything I need."

"Good night, Son."

"Good night, Dad."

Rig climbs the two sets of stairs to the attic. Rig's parents had converted the attic into a fully furnished family entertainment room during the first year they owned the house. Most of the rooms in the house are small. The attic stretches out to the full width and length of the house. All family gatherings, celebrations, and all entertaining occur in the third floor family room. The family room is the most comfortable room in the house. The rug is thicker and softer. Overstuffed chairs and sofas are conveniently positioned throughout the room. The room has a wet bar that is well stocked with scotch and bourbon. Two walls have custom-installed bay windows, which provide a spectacular view of the Naval Weapons Station dock, Anaheim Bay, the beach, and the Pacific Ocean.

Rig turns on the light. As he looks over the room, he reminisces about his high school girlfriends that he entertained in this room.

24

Seal Beach Café

Rig and his mother, Margaret Page, sit at a table in the front dining area of the Seal Beach café. He invited his mother to lunch so they could have some time alone to talk, away from the continuous visitors who are passing through their home this weekend to see Rig.

At his mother's insistence, Rig wears his Summer White uniform. His senior chief anchors gleam on his collar. Four rows of ribbons are pinned above his left breast pocket. His surface warfare insignia is pinned above his ribbons, and his submarine warfare insignia is pinned below his ribbons.

The man and woman who tail Rig entered the café five minutes after Rig and his mother entered; now those tails sit two tables away. The woman's large purse sits on the edge of the table and the purse's large ornate snap buckle points in Rig's direction.

Rig assumes there is a sensitive microphone and camera lens hidden in the purse buckle. He is confident that his tails do not know that he knows who they are.

The Seal Beach Café was Rig's high-school hangout. He and his friends would gather there after school and on weekends.

Fat Chad, the café owner, stands at the grill and cooks the best hamburgers in Seal Beach. Two second class petty officers from the Seal Beach Naval Weapons Station sit at the counter and wolf down *Chad Burgers*, the specialty of the cafe.

Rig stares appreciatively at Fat Chad and remembers the day he discovered that Fat Chad was a World War II submariner. All through high school, Fat Chad never talked about his past. Then, a decade ago Rig visited the café in uniform and Fat Chad revealed his past. Chad served as a torpedoman aboard a submarine during World War II. Chad showed Rig some pictures for those days onboard the World War II submarine that was home-ported in Pearl Harbor.

Chad's granddaughter, a fourteen-year-old with long shiny black hair and facial features that reflect her grandmother's native Hawaiian heritage, arrives at the table to take their order.

Rig and his mother order Chad Burgers.

While waiting for their food, Rig's mother

tells him about his father's current involvement in politics. "I'm surprised your father did not tell you what a bigwig he is in politics, now. He serves on several of Ronald Reagan's advisory committees and he organizes statewide fundraisers for Reagan's campaign. When Reagan was governor, Reagan called your father several times and asked for his advice on solving some political issues here in Orange County. Some are suggesting that your father run for state assembly."

Rig responds, "Politics is dad's passion. I'm glad he is pursuing his interests. For me, politics is boring."

Chad's granddaughter delivers their burgers.

While eating their lunch, Rig tells his mother about his European travels—leaving out the details of his undercover missions.

"No woman in your life?" his mother asks.

Images of Bella appear in his mind. "No one special, yet." Rig wants to avoid his romantic life being recorded by the people tailing him.

Ringing from the tiny bell mounted on the back of the café door causes Rig to look toward the door.

A tall, muscular black man wearing casual

163

summer slacks and polo shirt who appears the same age as Rig enters the café and walks toward the counter. When he sees Rigney Page sitting at a table, an enthusiastic smile appears on the man's face. He turns and approaches Rig's table.

Rig stands and extends his hand as he says, "Eddie, It's great to see you again!"

"Rig, you look fit!"

"So do you, Eddie. Working out?"

Eddie nods affirmative.

"Eddie, this is my mother, Margaret Page?"

Eddie takes Margaret's hand and says, "Very pleased to meet you, Mrs. Page."

Rig tells his mother, "Eddie and I were high school classmates. We played on several basketball teams together."

"A pleasure to meet you, Eddie," Margaret says with warm sincerity.

The young waitress comes to the table to take Eddie's order. He orders a BLT to go.

"Rig, I think the last time I saw you was in here ten years ago. You were on your way to Guam, if I am remembering correctly."

"Yes, Guam, ten years ago," Rig confirms. "Last I heard, you owned your own electrical contracting company. Is that right?"

"Yes. That's true."

"How's business?" Rig asks.

"I'm getting by," Eddie states. "The economy is in a slump right now."

"As you can see I am still in the navy and currently assigned to duty in San Diego."

"I was following your life in *The Long Beach Times* a couple of years ago," Eddie says, "but those articles about the mad bomber stopped not long after that reporter disappeared. Did the police give up on connecting your family to the disappearance of that reporter?"

Rig expresses curiosity while stating, "I haven't heard anything more about it since they searched my father's boat."

"I was on the dock that day when they searched your father's boat. The berth for my boat was directly across the dock from your father's.

"During the following week, there were several articles in *The Long Beach Times* saying that you and your father were persons of interest in Pyth's disappearance. The articles rehashed the feud between your family and Pyth over the Mad Bomber Case."

"The press is in partnership with the devil," Rig declares. "Do not believe what you read in newspapers."

Eddie asks, "What were they looking for on your father's boat?"

Rig answers, "They were searching for something that could be identified as belonging to Pyth and they were lifting fingerprints. They found neither."

Eddie asks, "So, you and your family have been cleared of any wrongdoing?"

"More like the Page family won and Pyth lost," Rig articulates.

Margaret Page expresses amusement at Rig's description.

In a tone dripping with contempt, Rig adds, "The Pyths of this world will always lose because their minds are enslaved by a destructive and failing ideology."

"Well said," Eddie appraises.

The waitress sets a brown paper bag in front of Eddie. He stands and hands her a five-dollar bill. "Keep the change," he tells her.

"Sorry to make this short," Eddie apologizes, "but I have an appointment. Hope to see you again soon."

After Eddie departs, Margaret Page comments, "I do not remember you ever talking about Eddie."

"Hmm, really."

A Jeep Cherokee stops at the curb outside of the café. The man who was called Eddie in the café enters the front passenger side of the Jeep.

Denton Phillips, Rig's Guardians contact, drives the Jeep north on Main Street.

Denton asks, "How'd it go, Larry?"

Larry Franklin expresses satisfaction as he reports, "Went exactly as you directed. If Pyth is the vengeful antagonist with a superiority complex that you say he is, Rig's words today and with his father last night should anger Pyth sufficiently to make him surface."

25

Temecula, California

The three-thousand-square-foot, Spanish-style ranch house sits in the center of a five acre section of hilly land fifty-miles north of San Diego. A security perimeter comprised of security cameras and motion detectors surrounds the ranch house at a distance of 300 feet. The ranch house had once served as a cell safehouse for the now defunct secret communist organization known as *The Longjumeau Alliance*.

Weston Pyth, alias Bill Owens, was the leader of that cell. When *The Longjumeau Alliance* fell apart due to its leaders being arrested by federal authorities, Pyth anticipated that the flow of support funds would discontinue. However, the bank in Switzerland that paid the mortgage, utilities, and repair costs during the active days of *The Longjumeau Alliance* continued to pay those expenses even after the alliance folded. Every month, Pyth submits bills to the Swiss bank and the bank pays them.

Pyth sits in the security room and listens to the voice taped conversations between Rigney Page and Page's father last Friday night. Then, he watches the video-taped conversation between Rigney Page and an old friend last Saturday afternoon in the Seal Beach Café.

An angry expression appears on his face as he declares, "That fascist bastard has my watch!"

Some of his anger derives from being involved in the Page family once again. He had thought he put all that behind him more than two years ago when he developed a plan to disappear and frame James Page for the disappearance.

But the watch was not found and Pyth now knows why. His anger at being out maneuvered feeds his desire for revenge.

For the frame to work, the police must find the watch in one of the Page's possession. Pyth begins to form a plan for that to happen.

26

Ocean Beach, San Diego

Weston Pyth, two of his own operatives, and a break-in specialist hired for this night's operation sit in a panel truck across the street from Rig's San Diego apartment building.

Pyth asks the specialist, "Are you sure you can access and search his apartment and leave no mark that you were there?"

"Yes," the specialist declares confidently. "Unless the resident knows we're coming and has set a trap or comes home unexpectedly."

"He doesn't know we're coming," Pyth affirms. "He's in Orange County for the weekend and will not return until tomorrow. You can take your time and search thoroughly. Take polaroid pictures of every watch you find, front and back as I explained before."

The specialist exits the vehicle. The footsteps of the tall and wiry specialist make no sound as he walks across the street.

One hour later, Pyth shifts around restlessly in the van. He glances at this watch—1:32 AM. "What's taking him so long?" he asks in a frustrating manner to no one in particular. His two operatives who sit in the front seat just shrug.

Several minutes later, the specialist opens the sliding door to the van. He steps in and sits next to Pyth.

"Randy, back to the motel," Pyth orders the driver.

"I did not find any watches," the specialist informs Pyth.

"Fuck!" Pyth vents in an angry tone.

After a few moments of silence, Pyth asks, "Anything of interest?"

"Considering this neighborhood, I expected to find an apartment furnished with quality, but that place is furnished like a cheap motel room. No memorabilia, no souvenirs, no files, no bills, no family pictures, and no personal belongings other what you would find in a suitcase. There were navy chief uniforms in the bedroom closet. I say that apartment is used more like a transient barracks than a long-term residence."

Pyth casts an inquiring expression at the specialist and asks, "You were in the navy?"

"Yes. Three years as a deck ape—first aboard a gator-freighter, then on a tin can."

Pyth does not understand what the

specialist just said but considers that the specialist's navy background may be useful in the future.

"What's next?" Randy asks from the driver's seat.

"Just some sleep for now," Pyth responds, frustration edging his tone.

27

Ocean Beach, San Diego

Rig drives off Interstate 8 and enters the Ocean Beach area of San Diego. He stops at a convenience store where he often buys gasoline for his car. After filling up, he goes to the pay phone and enters the number that will connect him to Denton Phillips.

"Hello," Denton answers.

"This is Rig. Did anything happen?"

"They searched your apartment early this morning. Pyth was there. We now have him under surveillance."

Rig senses finality in Denton's tone. He asks, "You have no more for me to do then?"

"Not at this time. We are grateful."

"What about my bodyguards?"

"Larry and his team will continue to guard you from a distance until this Pyth situation is over. You have Larry's contact number. Make sure you let him know if there is a sudden change to your schedule."

When Rig enters his apartment in Ocean Beach, he goes directly to the kitchen and pours two fingers of brandy into a snifter. A few minutes later, he sits in the dark on the apartment balcony and stares out toward the ocean.

His thoughts turn to his last mission in Italy when he met Bella. He hopes that she is safe in the CIA protection program. He wants to hear in her own voice that she is safe. During their last night together in Italy, they constructed a procedure she could use to contact him.

Please contact me soon, sweetheart.

28

Acey-Deucey Club
Naval Training Center San Diego

Rig sits in his car at the same spot in the Acey-Deucey Club parking lot as three previous evenings. He anticipates another boring evening waiting for the illusive Cleo to arrive. He turns on his transistor radio and hears Tom Jones asking, *'What's new, pussycat?'*

Shortly after the streetlights illuminate, car lights draw his attention the street. Cleo drives her car passed the parking lot and goes deeper into the base.

Rig has a dilemma. He was ordered by his controller not to tail Cleo. But he also understands that they had not considered Cleo would go anywhere else on the base. He starts his car.

As he follows Cleo, he keeps 200 feet behind her.

Cleo turns her car into the Chiefs Club parking lot.

Rig parks three rows behind where Cleo

parks.

Cleo exits her car; then, she stands in front of it. She wears a tight, figure-revealing, red evening dress with the hem slightly above the knees and a low-cut, cleavage-exposing neckline.

Rig notices movement at a car thee parking spaces to the left of Cleo's parking space. A tall, slim man in a Chief's Full Dress White uniform locks his car door. He walks to Cleo.

Cleo slips her arm under the chief's arm; they walk side by side into the Chiefs Club.

Rig feels confident that he can move around the parking lot without notice, he exits his vehicle with two radio beacons in hand. Attaching the beacons to the undersides of Cleo's car and the chief's car takes less than sixty seconds.

On the way home, he stops at a payphone and calls in a coded message to a recorder that radio beacons number one and two have been deployed as ordered.

Protocol requires that he wait three minutes on the phone after sending a coded message. His controller, Jeff Borden, comes on the line and tells Rig, "Meet me in my office at thirteen-hundred tomorrow. There has been a change to the next phase of your operation."

Thirty minutes later, Rig sits in the dark on his apartment balcony. He sips brandy and stares out over the two city blocks of neighborhood lights between him and the ocean. He contemplates his current situation.

He now regrets asking for a soft duty assignment. The fast-paced action of overseas missions stirs his memories of an exciting and adventurous life.

Starting tomorrow, he faces the excitement and adventure of a lesson plan audit conducted by the COMNAVEDTRA Inspection Team.

29

San Pedro Harbor
Los Angeles, California

Werner Braune and Weston Pyth sit at the bar in the main deck lounge aboard the *Paradisum*. They sip expensive brandy.

Werner Braune tells Pyth, "After you briefed me last week, I had the Page family investigated. James Page and his son are not easy targets. James Page won medals for bravery at the Battle of the Bulge. His military record labels him a hero. And his son Rigney led a group of sailors to overcome communist terrorists who attacked a navy base in Scotland. Rigney Page's military record calls him a hero.

"Both men are physically and mentally tough and they are courageous. The Page family lawyer is highly rated. The Pages are fighters and they always win. James Page organizes statewide fund raisers for Reagan and he sits on several of Reagan's advisory committees."

Pyth comments, "None of their strengths or James Page's power and influence will make a difference after I force them to come forward with the evidence. I already have the news articles drafted for Betsy's program that will prompt another investigation into Weston Pyth's disappearance."

Braune expresses doubt while he says, "What if law enforcement determines there is not enough evidence for another investigation?"

Pyth casts a knowing smile. "It's not law enforcement that has to be convince of criminal activity. It's the voter that needs convincing, and I can keep the allegations going in the newspapers until after the election. Considering the timeline, grand juries would probably not convene until after the election. Remember, our objective in this Page operation is to prevent Reagan from being elected by showing voters that the Reagan campaign consists of lawless oppressors. If the Pages are found guilty later, consider that a plus for future elections.

"We can adapt the Page operation to frame other influential members of the Reagan campaign. Time is short for the Page operation; so we need to use your yacht. Future operations will be adapted so that use of your yacht is not necessary.

Braune shakes his head and expresses revelation. "Political sabotage is a science all in its own. I never realized."

"I can go forward, then?" Pyth asks in an anxious tone. Pyth desperately needs Braune's support and agreement on this radical plan against the Pages; because, mostly, Pyth needs Braune's protection if the plan fails.

Braune is hesitant because his yacht is an integral element in Pyth's brutal plan. But, then, this would not be the first time his yacht was the platform for brutal acts.

Braune knows that his yacht is the safest place to conduct the Page operation because he trusts his crew not to reveal events aboard the yacht. His crew is loyal to him. Most of the crew have criminal records in their home countries and were unemployable; but Braune hired them anyway. He pays the crew three-times the competitive salary for yacht crewmen. He also pays their medical needs and allows two-week paid vacations every year. When a crewman assists Braune in a nefarious act, that crewman receives a generous bonus. What happens on the *Paradisum* is hidden from the world.

The crew also knows that there is severe punishment for those who commit disloyal acts. Each crewman remembers two occasions when crewmen were disloyal to Braune. Those crewman disappeared and were never heard from again.

Although Owens has been very busy and has spent millions of dollars, the approval poll numbers between Carter and Reagan have narrowed, not widened. The press prints constant negatives every day about Ronald Reagan; yet, poll numbers do not reflect the negatives.

The Trajan Consortium Board pressures Braune to produce something that will push Carter twenty points ahead in the polls. Members of *The Trajan Consortium*, including Braune, could lose billions of Mideast oil dollars if Ronald Reagan wins.

Braune tells Pyth, "Proceed with your plan."

"And the stateroom?" Pyth asks.

"I will have the engineer make the security changes you requested."

181

30

The Holiday Inn on Rosecrans
San Diego, California

Rig enters Denton's hotel room. Larry Franklin sits in a chair across the room.

Rig takes a chair next to Larry.

Denton sits on the edge of the bed, facing Rig and Larry.

"Brace yourself, Rig," Denton warns. "I have some disturbing information that is personal to you."

"What is it?" Rig asks calmly.

"Pyth kidnapped your sister, Terri."

Rig jumps up from the edge of the bed, expressing horror. "When?! How?! Are you sure?! Is she okay?!"

"Yesterday morning, we were tracking one of Pyth's teams when they drove into a grocery store parking lot. They pulled up behind your sister's car. When she exited her car, they grabbed her, put a hood over her head, and threw her in the backseat of their car."

"Did they hurt her?!"

"My operatives followed them to San Pedro

Harbor where they took her aboard a yacht named the *Paradisum*. My operatives reported she did not look harmed."

"Why didn't they rescue her?!" Rig challenges loudly in a demanding tone.

"Calm down, Rig," Denton says in an unruffled tone. "The kidnapping occurred without warning. My operatives following Pyth's team do not know about you or your family. Remember, we are cell organization. Like you, *Guardian* operatives are trained not to react impulsively to sudden situation changes. Plus, they did not know what the situation was. The prime directive is to never reveal *The Guardians* exist.

Rig appears puzzled.

"My operatives traced the license plate number on your sister's car. That's how we found out who was kidnapped. Actually, we have discovered a lot during the last twenty-four hours."

"I must call my parents."

"Not a good idea," Denton specifies. "The less people that know about this the better. A careless release of such information could destroy our rescue plan."

"But won't they contact my parents with their

demands?"

"Not yet," Denton asserts, "and probably not until next week. Obviously, the kidnapping is to lure you and your father into a trap that probably connects you and your father to Pyth's disappearance several years ago."

Rig sits back down and inquires, "What makes you think they will not move until next week?"

"Give me a chance to explain," Denton says calmly. "This morning, the *Paradisum* moved from its dock in San Pedro to an anchorage at Catalina Island where it will spend the weekend. This Saturday night there is a rich, elitist social event at a mansion on the island. With that on Braune's schedule and with the *Paradisum* at anchor at Catalina, their plan to notify you must be early next week. They probably believe that by then your family will be frantic with fear and will act impulsively to any demand. We will execute a rescue plan before that—early Sunday morning."

"I hope you are including me in that plan?" Rig challenges.

"Yes, of course," Denton answers "You and Larry."

Denton explains, "They made a tactical

mistake in believing they were not in someone's sights. Taking your sister to that yacht has allowed *The Guardians* to connect a lot of dots leading to *The Trajan Consortium*. That yacht, the *Paradisum*, is owned by Werner Braune."

"The movie producer?!" Larry questions in a surprised tone. "The one who made that disgusting movie, *Last Flag Standing*?"

"Yes. That's him," Denton affirms. "*The Guardians* first suspected him to be a key figure in *The Trajan Consortium* about two years ago."

In an incredulous tone, Larry states, "They say that movie is destined to be awarded movie of the year at the Oscars. Hollywood has gone nuts."

"Back on topic, please!" Rig blurts in an impatient, loud tone.

"We are developing a plan to rescue her and sabotage *The Trajan Consortium* at the same time."

"Why not sooner than early Sunday morning?" Rig asks.

"Only the duty section will be aboard the *Paradisum* Saturday night. That situation allows an easy approach to the *Paradisum* whore your sister is being held captive.

"I have chartered a flight from San Diego to Catalina Island for you two and three other operatives. Be at Montgomery Field at noon on Saturday. I will pick you up at the Catalina airport and take you to a cabin cruiser that will serve as our operations center."

"I'm impressed," Larry claims, "You obtained a lot of information in only twenty-four hours."

"We have an inside informer. We bought a *Paradisum* crewmember. He became highly motivated to assist us when we told him he can become rich or he can become dead."

Rig is startled; he questions, "*The Guardians* have not become cold blooded killers of the innocent; have they?"

"Of course not," Denton affirms. "We bluffed him, and he bought it."

Rig asks, "Will Pyth and this Braune be onboard when we go aboard to rescue my sister?"

"I don't know," Denton answers, "They were both onboard when the yacht departed San Pedro. According to our crew insider, only the duty section will be aboard Saturday night."

Knowing that Denton has an inside informer causes Rig to feel confident in Denton's assessment and rescue plan.

Rig asks Denton, "Whatever other objectives you have regarding Braune and Pyth, rescuing my sister is number one priority, right?"

"Absolutely, Rig," Denton responds with total sincerity. "You will see that when I brief you and the others on the assault plan Saturday afternoon."

31

Avalon Bay, Catalina Island
Onboard the Cabin Cruiser, *Frigg*

Denton, Rig, and Larry stand on one side of the dining table. The three operatives who will serve as backup assault team stand on the other side of the table. The galley area of the fifty-feet-long *Frigg* provides more than enough space for the six men.

Denton starts the briefing. "The *Paradisum* crewman who stole these design diagrams checked off duty this morning. He planted the bomb inside the main power distribution panel before leaving the yacht.

"The ship's engineer is ashore but could go aboard tomorrow morning; so, the earliest that the missing diagrams could be noticed is tomorrow morning. Meaning that you must complete the operation during the early morning dark hours."

Denton lays out the first design diagram. "The *Paradisum* engineering spaces are located in the aft third of the ship and occupies the bottom two levels. They are the largest spaces on the ship with no watertight doors between them. The bottom level is totally beneath the waterline. This is a diagram of the bottom level of the engineering spaces. When the yacht is at anchor, there is always one crewman on watch in the engineering spaces."

Denton points to where the two screw shafts pass through the hull. "Larry, the thinnest area of the hull is near the screw shafts, here."

"Got it," Larry responds.

Denton replaces the engineering diagram with a topside deck diagram and explains, "When the ship is docked or at anchor, access to the interior of the yacht is controlled through one doorway near the gangway. All other doors to the outside decks are lock and monitored with electrical sensors.

"There is a security room on the O-1 level . . . here, adjacent to the radio room. The security watch monitors all security sensors and a camera system that views the gangway, bow, and helicopter deck.

Our insider says that at 2:00 AM the security room watch, the armed roving watch, and the armed gangway watch should be the only crewman on or above the main deck. Rig, your sister is locked in a guest stateroom next to the owner's stateroom on the main deck . . . here.

The roving watch circles the main deck and randomly circles the 0-1 and 0-2 levels. When the camera systems show a boat approaching the gangway, the security room watch uses the yacht's announcing system to order the roving watch to the gangway for added security.

"The bomb in the power panel is set to go off at 2:00 AM tomorrow morning. Stay in your launches and beyond the illumination of the yacht's lights until the yacht's power fails and the emergency lanterns come on. We won't know how much light we will have to operate until those lanterns come on.

"All of you will be dressed in black coveralls, black bulletproof vests, black gloves, and black tactical hoods. The tactical hoods have holes only for your eyes so that minimum facial features are exposed. You will be equipped with automatic pistols and automatic rifles, all with suppressors. Your clothes and equipment are in the berthing area.

"We will all be on the same radio frequency. All of you will wear microphone headsets. Rig and Larry in Launch One are call sign *Team One*. The backup team will be in Launch Two and have the call sign *Team Two*. I will be callsign *Control*.

"The entire duty section, except for the gangway watch, roving watch, and security room watch will be investigating the cause of the power outage and working on repair in the engine room. So there will be two armed bad guys topside. The gangway watch and roving watch have orders to open fire on anyone attempting to board the yacht from any conveyance other than the yacht's own motor launch."

"What about Braune and Pyth?" Rig asks.

"Braune will not be aboard. He checked into the same hotel where the event he is attending tonight. Pyth was aboard when *Paradisum* sailed from San Pedro. He could be aboard tonight."

Denton waits for more questions; none arise. He continues the briefing. "When the main electrical power fails. All electric controlled security locks will fail to the *unlocked* position. The only lighting will be provided by battery powered emergency lanterns. The stateroom where Rig's sister is confined has a manual sliding bolt lock on the passageway side of the door."

"Where are the launches we will be using?"

asks one of the backup team.

"They will be delivered here about midnight," Denton answers. "The weather forecast for tonight calls for mild sea swells and ten-mile-per-hour winds. The launches will be heavy enough to easily maneuver in that weather condition."

Rig interrupts. "Are you certain your insider planted that bomb?"

"I am certain. He believes his life depends on it."

"Where is the insider now?" Larry asks.

"We have him bound and gagged and under guard. If the bomb goes off at 2:00 AM, he will be released tomorrow morning a rich man."

Rig exhibits confidence in Denton's words.

Denton continues the briefing. He points at the diagrams as he explains the assault plan.

32

Avalon Bay, Catalina Island

Rig stands in the aft area of Launch One; Larry sits at the helm in the middle of the launch. They watch the 300-foot-long *Paradisum* from a distance of 50 yards, beyond the illumination cast by the yacht's lights. Launch Two is ten yards distant from Launch One. The idling motors of the two launches blend with the sounds of the harbor. A mild wind and mild sea state causes minor pitch and roll for the two launches.

Denton sits at the radio in the cabin cruiser, *Frigg*, and listens to reports by the two teams.

They all await for the power failure that has been set for 2:00 AM. The gangway watch is clearly visible under the lights of the *Paradisum* gangway deck.

A thundering noise comes from within the yacht. Lights and equipment shut off throughout the yacht.

Twenty-three electric-powered door locks fail to the *unlocked* position. Because of a nonexistent preventative maintenance program for backup systems, only ono third of emergency, battery-powered lanterns power on.

The Uninterruptible Power Supply (UPS) unit in the Security Center provides power to the security camera systems; but because two-thirds of the emergency lights do not power on, the security cameras can see only a few spots on the bow. The deck area at the top of the gangway and the gangway itself are dark.

The press-to-transmit switch for the radio is on Rig's belt, as it is for every member of the two teams. Rig presses the switch and speaks into the radio microphone, "This is Team One Leader; something went wrong on the yacht. Only a few emergency lights are lit on the main deck. The gangway deck and the gangway itself are dark. All topside decks are mostly dark, making our boarding plan unworkable."

After a short pause, Rig orders over the radio. "This is Team One Leader; everyone strap on your night-vision monocular."

Rig looks through his night-vision monocular. "This is Team One Leader; the gangway watch is standing fast." Rig scans the rest of the starboard side. "I do not see anyone else. The roving watch can be anywhere."

Denton's voice comes over the radio. "Team One Leader, this is Control; take charge and construct a new assault plan. Time is not on our side."

Rig must now rely on his training, experience, and instinct to successively complete this operation. After a short pause for quick planning, Rig advises over the radio, "This is Team One leader; I will attempt to get the gangway watch to surrender. I will keep my operation to the starboard side. Team Two, station your launch twenty yards off the yacht's starboard side. Tell me when you are in place. Aim one rifle at the gangway watch. Use the other two rifles to scan the starboard side for the rover. Take them down if they starts shooting."

Rig hears over the radio, "This is Team Two Leader; roger WILCO."

Rig tells Larry, "Place us ten feet off the gangway. If shooting starts, move us quickly toward the yacht's bow. Keep our distance to the yacht a constant ten feet. I do not want us crashing in to Launch Two."

As Launch One nears the gangway, Rig sees that the gangway watch appears curious as to the source of the approaching motors.

The gangway watch is expecting an order over the announcement system for the rover to report to the gangway, but the order does not come. Then, he realizes the power outage has probably turned off the cameras and announcing system. He knows there are no arrivals scheduled during his watch, but something is approaching. He has never been trained for this situation. He becomes unsure as to what he should do.

"Team One Leader, this is Team Two Leader; Launch Two is in place and rifles aimed as you directed."

Larry shifts Launch One's throttle to the idle position. The launch bobs slightly in a light swell and in the dark ten feet from the gangway.

The gangway watch hears the sound of a close by motor slowing to a steady idle. He knows it is close but cannot see it. Now believing that something unusual is happening, he pulls his pistol but holds it at his side.

"This is Team Two Leader; gangway watch has pulled his pistol and holds it at his side."

Rig picks up his rifle. He lifts his night-vision monocular away from his face; then looks through the night-vision scope on the rifle. He places the crosshairs over the heart of the gangway watch.

Rig yells out, "You on the *Paradisum.* Two rifles are aimed at your heart. Drop your weapon in the water and come down the gangway. If you comply, you will live."

The rover walks out to the starboard side twenty feet aft of the gangway. He hears Rig's warning.

Fast and loud over the radio: "Rover on deck! He has a machine pistol! He is firing into the water!"

At the sound of gunfire, Larry engages Launch One's throttle and speeds toward the yacht's bow. Rig puts down his rifle; then places his night-vision monocular over his eyes.

Launch Two fires a barrage of bullets at the rover.

The gangway watch raises his pistol and starts firing toward the water where he sees flashes of gunfire.

Six bullets tear through the rover's body, one bullet to the middle of his face. The rover falls dead to the deck.

The gangway watch takes two bullets to his chest and two to his head. He falls dead to the deck

No one in Teams One and Two are hit with gunfire.

"This is Team Two Leader; both the gangway watch and rover are down, probably dead but be careful."

Rig says over the radio, "This is Team One leader; I am going up the gangway. Cover me."

Rig tells Larry, "Take us to the gangway."

Team Two has their rifles aimed at the starboard side. The burst of bullets they fired were silenced by suppressors. However, the gun fire from the yacht was not suppressed and loud enough to be heard inside the yacht's superstructure. More armed men might come topside to investigate.

As Launch One closes the distance to the gangway, Rig takes inventory of his assault supplies. He wears an ammo vest over his bulletproof vest. The ammo vest contains tools and ammunition he will need while onboard. He moves his hands from one pouch to the other and confirms he as three spare magazines for his .9mm Beretta, a flashlight and spare batteries, two concussion grenades, a combat knife, and assorted small tools.

Rig easily maneuvers the jump from the

launch to the gangway platform. He pulls his Beretta and screws on the suppressor; then aims upward toward the top of the gangway. Rig advances up the gangway two steps at a time.

Larry maneuvers Launch One away from the gangway; then drives toward the stern.

At the top of the gangway, Rig verifies that the gangway watch is dead. "This is Team One Leader; the gangway watch is dead," Rig drags the body to the rail and pushes the body overboard.

Rig walks aft and finds the dead body of the rover. He reports the dead body over the radio; then pushes the rover's body overboard.

Launch Two takes Launch One's place at the bottom of the gangway.

According to the diagrams of the main deck, Rig's sister is locked in a stateroom amidship. He memorized the path to the stateroom earlier in the day.

Rig opens a door to the amidships passageway. Through the night-vision monocular, he sees an illuminated emergency light at the other end of the passageway. The emergency light casts a glare through the night-vision monocular; he flips up the monocular away from his eyes.

The emergency light provides enough illumination to view the passageway. He keeps his Beretta at the ready.

Rig knows from the main deck diagram and from the insider's information that the main salon is on his left and Braune's stateroom is on the right. The stateroom that holds his sister is the stateroom next to Braune's.

Rig is relieved to see that the twelve-inch sliding bolt lock on the stateroom door is not secured with a padlock. Unknown to Rig is that the sliding bolt lock was an added security measure at Pyth's request when the stateroom was selected to hold Terri Page. Since the bolt lock can only be operated from the passageway side, Pyth saw no reason to add a padlock.

Quietly, Rig slides the bolt, turns the doorknob, and pushes the door open. Light from the passageway emergency lantern radiates through the stateroom door and provides enough illumination to see inside.

Terri Page is asleep on the bed. She is fully clothed and lies on top of the bed covers.

Rig shakes her shoulder as he calls out to her. "Terri, wake up!"

Terri opens her eyes, expressing surprise; then, expressing fear as she sees a person wearing a hood and a strange looking device strapped to his head. She squirms away across the bed.

"Terri, it's me, Rig. I am here to rescue you."

Terri recognizes Rig's voice and responds, "What? How did . . . what's going on?"

"Are you okay?" Rig asks. "Did they harm you in any way?"

"They didn't harm me. What's going on?!"

"No time to answer questions. I have a boat waiting." He hands her a small flashlight. "Put on your shoes, hold on to my belt, and follow me. Bring with you anything that could show you were ever aboard."

"There is nothing," Terri responds. "Oh, wait my fingerprints."

"Your fingerprints will not be a problem. Let's go."

As they walk along the passageway toward the starboard side, Rig says into the radio, "This is Team One Leader; I have the target, and we are moving toward the gangway."

"Who are you talking to," Terri asks.

"Your transportation."

Rig lowers the night-vision monocular over

his eyes."

When they reach the bottom of the gangway, Rig assists his sister into Launch Two.

Terri's expresses astonished bewilderment as she sees three men in the launch dressed exactly the same as her brother.

"These are my friends," he tells Terri. "They will protect you and take you to a boat on the other side of the anchorage. You will be safe there. I will join you within the hour."

"But where are you going?!" Her tone filled with anxiety.

"No questions, now. Later." Rig goes back up the gangway.

As Rig climbs the ladder to the 01 level, he says into the radio, "Launch One, where are you?"

"Moving toward the gangway," Larry responds over the radio."

"Launch One, did you deliver the package?"

"Affirmative. Package delivered," Larry responds.

As Rig approaches the 01 level, he sees that the passageway leading to the security center is illuminated with emergency lighting. The insider's briefing advised the yacht had no inside cameras; so, Rig is not concerned with being detected before entering the security room.

Rig verifies the Beretta safeties are off. He opens the security room door. He expects to encounter the security room watch. The security room is brightly illuminated.

A medium sized man with sandy colored hair and beard, puffing on a cigarette, sits at the desk staring at a video screen. He speaks into a microphone for the yacht's announcing system. "Roving watch, report to security." But the announcing system is not working.

The man's left side is toward Rig. He turns his head casually to see who is entering. When he sees a tall person wearing black from head to toe pointing a suppressor-equipment automatic pistol at him, he expresses fear.

Rig orders, "Put out the cigarette; then, stand and raise your hands! Disobey and you die!"

The security room watch complies. When the man stands, Rig notes that the man is flabby with a paunch.

"Move and inch and you die!" Rig warns.

The sound of a computer printer comes from the radio room.

Rig nods toward the open doorway that leads to the radio room. "Is there anyone in there? Lie and you die."

"No one," the man states in a weak and fearful voice.

Rig casts a doubtful look at the security watch.

The security watch explains, "I'm the radio room watch. In port, the radio room watch doubles as the security room watch."

Rig detects a Germanic accent in the man's voice. "Are you German?" Rig inquires.

"Austrian," the man responds.

Rig moves toward the radio room doorway; he keeps his Beretta aimed at the man's chest. Rig glances into the radio room several times for a split second each time, not giving the security watch enough time to make an advantageous move. Powered up receivers, transmitters, and printers stand along three walls. File cabinets line the fourth wall. He notes the file cabinets are secured with padlocks.

"What is providing power to these two rooms?"

"UPS equipment," the security man replies. "One in this room and two in the radio room."

"How many crewmembers are aboard tonight and where are they?"

"Eleven. There is me and two guards topside. The rest are in the engine room fixing the power problem."

"Is Mr. Braune aboard or any passengers?"

"Mr. Braune is not aboard. He is scheduled to return Monday morning. Mr. Owens and a woman whose name I do not know are only passengers onboard."

Rig recognizes *Owens* as Weston Pyth's alias.

"Where is Mr. Owens?"

"I believe he is asleep in his stateroom. But with the ventilation system shutdown, his stateroom will become uncomfortable. He will probably wake up and go out to the weather deck. It won't take long for him to realize something is wrong and come up here."

"Where are the keys to those file cabinets?"

"Mr. Owens has them."

Rig asks, "Do you have a life vest handy?"

"Yes, in that locker." The security watch nods toward a metal locker in the corner."

"Put it on; slowly. You will survive this incident because we want you to tell your story about this event, fully and honestly. Do not fear reprisal."

After the man has strapped on the life vest, Rig nods toward the passageway door and says, "We are going out to the weather deck on the starboard side. You walk ahead of me. Do not attempt to overcome me. I will put two bullets into your heart before you move two inches in the wrong direction. Move!"

At the rail on the 0-1 level weather deck, Rig says to the security watch, "Do you see that boat at the bottom of the gangway?"

"Barely."

"Similar boats surround this yacht. I am giving you a chance to live. Do not attempt to come back aboard or you will be shot. I recommend you swim toward those lights. That's the closest land. Now jump."

The man's splash is heard by both Rig and Larry.

Rig reports over the radio, "Security room watch in the water with a life vest."

Putting the security watch in the water with a life vest so he could tell his story to authorities was part of the original assault plan.

Rig enters the superstructure and walks toward the security room. He pauses with caution when he sees a moving shadow cast from the security room across passageway. He glances at the port side door to the passageway and concludes that door was the person's access point.

Rig slows his movement toward the open security room door. He brings his Beretta to the ready position.

Weston Pyth stands at the security office desk and stares at the three security displays that should show brightly illuminated decks but display dark. He puts it all together: power failure, emergency lighting failures, missing gangway watch, missing rover watch, missing security room watch, and what sounded like gun shots some minutes ago. He concludes hostile forces could be aboard.

Pyth hears movement coming from the passageway. *How can I defend myself!*

He becomes frantic looking for a place to hide; there is no hiding space. Then, he remembers the pistol kept in the top left-hand desk drawer. Instinct causes him to open the drawer and retrieve a large automatic pistol.

Pyth does not know the pistol's caliber nor does he know how to use it. His ideology believes that private gun ownership is an afront to civilized society; only the police and the military should possess guns. So, he never learned how to use guns.

Pyth points the gun at the open doorway and hopes the gun will fire when he pulls the trigger.

Most of Rig's body is hidden behind the bulkhead as he makes a quick peek in to the security room. He sees a person pointing a gun at the open doorway.

Pyth glimpses a person wearing a ski mask. Frightened, he shifts the gun's aim toward the ski mask. He attempts to pull the trigger; the gun does not fire.

Instinctively, Rig fires three shots toward the man. Then he hides behind the bulkhead. He hears what he believes to be a body falling to the deck.

He takes another quick peek. The man is lying in the deck. The gun lies on the deck a few feet away.

Rig is not confident the man is disabled. He believes his first and third shots missed and does not know how damaging the second shot was.

Rig enters the security office with his pistol aimed at the man's head. He stoops and picks up the man's gun. Rig expresses curiosity when he sees the firing safety in the safe position.

Blood pumps from the man's chest and spreads over the deck. Rig recognizes the man as Weston Pyth from pictures Denton showed him earlier.

Rig quickly examines Pyth. He believes he feels a faint pulse but is not sure. He concludes that Pyth is immobilized and if not dead will bleed to death in a few minutes. Pyth is no longer a threat.

Rig wastes a few moments staring at the onetime *Long Beach Times* reporter and current domestic terrorist who has caused the Page family so much pain and suffering.

Rig searches Pyth's body for keys to the file cabinets. He finds a keyring on Pyth's belt. He sighs relief knowing that he will not need to eat time by using his lockpick set or prying off the padlock hasps.

In the radio room. He pulls off all the frequency lists taped to the sides of radio equipment and stuffs them into his backpack.

Although there are three four-drawer filing cabinets, they hold only a total of thirty-seven file folders and code books. Rig stuffs all the files and code books into the backpack.

Rig turns off the radio room UPS units. The radio room goes dark. He cuts all the power cords connected to the UPS units.

In the security room, Rig checks Pyth's condition. Pyth is dead. Rig stares at Pyth's dead body and concludes justice has been dealt.

Denton's voice comes over the radio: "Team One Leader this is Control; you are three minutes behind schedule."

On his way out the security room door, Rig reports. "Control and Launch One, this is Team One Leader. I will be at the gangway in thirty-seconds." He dashes from the security room and heads for the gangway.

Five minutes later, Launch One with Rig and Larry aboard is fifty-yards distant from the yacht. The launch motor is idling. They both watch the yacht through their night-vision monocular. Rig sits in the bow of the launch. Larry sits in the middle at the wheel. They both stare in the direction of the yacht *Paradisum*.

A rumbling sound rolls across the water; then a geyser of water shoots up from the stern of the yacht.

The underwater explosive package that Larry put in place was designed to blow out a ships shaft seals and crack the hull around the shafts. The flooding is fast enough to overcome bilge pumps, but slow enough so crew and passengers can abandon ship with time to spare.

Nothing moves for ten minutes. Then, the yacht shows a slight down angle on the stern.

"Down angle on the stern," Rig reports over the radio.

As the minutes pass, the down angle on the stern quickens. When there is a twenty degree down angle, crewmembers appear on the main deck with safety vests and rubber rafts.

Rig counts eight people jump into the water, board rubber rafts, and paddle toward the closest shore.

"She's going down fast, now," Rig reports over the radio.

Control orders over the radio, "Launch One, return home."

Larry engages the launch's motor and turns the launch in the direction of the cabin cruiser, *Frigg*.

33

Cabin Cruiser, *Frigg*
Avalon Bay, Catalina Island

Rig and Larry remove their tactical hoods as they enter the galley.

Terri Page, Denton Philips, and one of the Team Two members sit at the table and sip coffee.

Terri Page jumps to her feet and hugs her brother. "Rig, what's going on?!" She demands. "No one is telling me anything! And why are you dressed like that?! A gun?! A knife?! Are those hand grenades?!"

"Hold on, Terri. I need to remove all this equipment."

Rig and Larry go to the berthing area and remove their ammo vests, bullet proof vest, and handguns. They lay the equipment and weapons on their bunks. Rig stores the two hand grenades in the grenade locker. They return to the galley.

Denton offers, "Sit down and have some coffee." Denton pours two cups of coffee and slides the cups toward two empty seats.

Rig responds to his sister's previous questions, "Okay, Terri, I will tell you as much as I can."

After everyone settles at the table, Rig smiles at his sister and asks, "Do you remember Weston Pyth?"

"Yes, he's that *Long Beach Times* reporter who said horrible things about you and Dad in the newspaper. He disappeared a year or so ago. The police questioned Dad and searched Dad's boat."

Rig briefs his sister on Pyth's recent past. "Pyth went underground. He became a paid organizer for political sabotage. He assumed an alias name, Bill Owens. When he went underground, he used that situation as an opportunity to frame Dad for murder. Pyth planted evidence on Dad's boat to make it look like Dad killed Pyth and dumped the body in the sea.

"Recently, Pyth teamed with international oligarchs to destroy Ronald Reagan's campaign for president. That yacht where you were held hostage belongs to one of those oligarchs, Werner Braune."

"The movie producer?!" Terri expresses shock.

"Yes."

"I was in two of his movies." Terri expresses astonishment.

Rig pauses to sip coffee.

"How did I get involved in all this?" Terri asks in a calmer tone. "And how are you involved in all this? I mean, you're dressed like and act like a commando."

Rig explains, "Dad is an influential bigwig in Reagan's California campaign. We believe Pyth kidnapped you to force Dad to do something scandalous. Something that would damage our family's reputation and damage Reagan's image."

"How are Mom and Dad handling me being kidnapped?"

"They don't know." Rig answers, "and my plan is that they never find out. We are going to get you back to your apartment before your weekly Sunday night call to Mom. I need you to keep all this a secret."

Terry expresses confusion. "Then how did you know I was kidnapped and know where they held me?"

Denton speaks up. "We had Pyth's organization under surveillance. One of my operatives reported that they abducted a woman. We ran a check on the car license number, and your named popped up. We contacted Rig immediately, then we organized your rescue."

"Who are you?" Terri asks staring curiously at Denton.

"I cannot tell your that, Terri. There is a larger situation in which we are involved that must be kept secret. I ask you not to tell anyone about your abduction and rescue."

"Oh my god, you're secret agents!" She casts and astonishing stare at Rig and asks, "Does Dad and Mom know?"

Rig shakes his head.

No one corrects Terri's speculation. They are satisfied with her thinking they are secret agents.

Then, in a concerned manner, Terri asks, "What's to stop those men from abducting me again?"

"Pyth is dead," Rig informs, "and Braune will be warned to stay away from our family."

"You killed Pyth?!" Terri asks in a shocked tone.

"He brought it upon himself. He pointed a gun at me."

Terri shakes her head in disbelief over what

her brother has become. "I thought you were just a sailor."

"Please never tell anyone that I am anything else."

"Where is Pyth's body?" Denton asks.

"On the deck in the security room, submerged," Rig answers.

Terry asks, "What about Mr. Braune? He knows who I am, and he knows that I know about him."

"Werner Braune will be leaving the country soon," Denton informs. "A note will arrive with his room service breakfast tray later this morning. The note will demand he leave the United States within 24 hours and never come back or he will suffer the same fate as Bill Owens. The note will also tell him to stay out of American politics or suffer the same fate as Bill Owens. He will also be warned that should any physical or financial harm come to any member of the *Paradisum* crew or any member of the Page family he will suffer the same fate as Bill Owens.

"Braune will know that Owens spent the night on the yacht. When Braune reads our note, he will go to his hotel room balcony to see if his yacht exhibits any abnormally. He will

216

become frightened when he looks out toward the harbor and sees that his yacht is missing. Later in the day, he will learn that his yacht was sunk and that Mr. Owens and the woman passenger are missing.

"Within twenty-four hours, we will conduct another attack on Braune's organization—an action to validate that our threat against him is real.

"Days from now when Pyth's body is found inside the sunken yacht and newspapers report that he was shot to death, Braune will know our threat against him is serious."

"Won't he already know about his yacht by Breakfast time," Terry questions.

Denton glances at his watch. "It's 4:15 and there has been no chatter on harbor radio about anything unusual. It will take most of the morning before harbor authorities discover the *Paradisum* has sunk at anchor. Then, harbor management will check its records and discover that the *Paradisum* is registered to a company that is a subsidiary of a large European corporation. They will attempt to contact management of that company on a Sunday morning."

Terri Page says in a weak, cracking voice,

"All of this is so terrifying."

Rig puts his arm around his sister and pulls her close. Rig feels remorseful, again, for placing his family in danger. His debt to *The Guardians* for protecting his family is incalculable. He recommits to serve *The Guardians* honestly and fully as long as he can.

Denton asks, "Terri, can I count on you to never mention this abduction incident and what you have learned about Werner Braune?"

Terri looks toward Rig.

Rig nods.

"Yes," Terri answers.

The *Frigg*'s engines roar to life and the cabin cruiser gains speed.

Denton tells Terri, "We will dock at Marina Del Rey in four hours. There will be a car waiting to take you home. Rig will accompany you. We retrieved your car and parked it in front of your apartment building."

34

Avalon Grand Hotel
Catalina Island

Werner Braune opens the door to his hotel suite and allows the bellman to push the breakfast table into the room.

The bellman rolls the table to the center of the suite's sitting room. He removes the cloth and exposes a continental breakfast and one hotplate with a metal cover.

Braune adds a tip to the bill and signs it. The bellman departs.

He pours a cup of coffee; then lifts the metal lid from the plate of heated muffins. He sees a small white envelope wedged between the two muffins. He pulls a note from the envelope.

After reading the note, Braune walks out to the balcony and looks over the harbor to where he expects to see his yacht. The *Paradisum* is not there. He quickly scans the harbor but does not see the *Paradisum.*

Back in the sitting room, Werner Braune picks up the telephone handset and dials a room number. Braune's VP for Special Projects answers.

"Send Franklyn to find the *Paradisum*," Braune orders the VP. "Have him start with the harbor master."

"What happened?" the VP asks in a surprised tone.

"I don't know. The *Paradisum* is not in the harbor. I want a report by noon."

"Yes, Mr. Braune."

Werner sits down at the mobile breakfast table. His coffee is still hot enough to drink. He butters a muffin.

35

Switzerland

The two operatives hide in a heavily wooded area one-hundred-and-fifty yards from *Le Haut Château*. The time is 11:30 PM; they have been there since just before sunset. Each hold night-vision binoculars to their eyes. They can easily see the two rampart style towers on the northeast corner and southwest corners of the château. Security lights on top of the towers make the towers easy targets. Security cameras atop each tower provide total perimeter coverage for the château.

One of the operatives speaks into a portable, high-frequency transceiver. "Control this is Foxtrot. We are in position and ready to deliver the message."

"This is Control. Deliver the message."

Each operative has a LAW Rocket Launcher slung over his shoulder. They go through the pre-firing procedure; then, they take aim on the rampart towers. One operative takes aim on the north tower, and the other operative takes aim on the south tower.

"Fire on zero," one of the men orders. "Four, three, two, one, zero." They both push the trigger on their individual launcher. Each rocket's fire trail allow the operatives to follow the rockets to their targets.

Several seconds later, explosions blow apart the top of the five-century-old towers and destroy the towers' security lighting and cameras.

36

Radioman Schools
NTC San Diego

The COMNAVEDTRA inspector tells Rig, "Senior Chief, a review of the student critique sheet file has some lesson-plan critiques that have no resolution recorded."

"Can I see them, please?" Rig asks.

Rig thumbs through the critiques. "Those critiques do not list complete references or don't list references at all. When that happens, we just file them without action."

"Why don't you go back to the students and ask them to provide complete references?"

"Because the critique form already specifies that references are required and must include manual title, page number, and paragraph number. We make that a requirement to avoid students making a critique based on opinions instead of valid references."

The inspector opines, "But to ignore critiques because they're incorrectly submitted discourages subordinates from contributing."

Rig stares at the civilian contract inspector

whose I.D. card specifies him as a GS-11 equivalent. Rig has become very annoyed at this nit-picking inspection team who has been on his ass for the past two weeks.

Unlike inspection teams he has experienced in the past, including those when he was an inspector, this COMNAVEDTRA Inspection Team is long on opinions and short on references.

Rig responds, "I will send these critiques sheets back to the students with a note to include complete references."

"I will note that on the inspection sheet," the inspector informs.

After the inspector departs, Rig decides to go for some coffee. As he walks to the instructors lounge, he compares the impact of his actions last weekend in Catalina to his current soft duty assignment. He confirms to himself that conquering evil globalists face to face impacts the world significantly more than surveillance at a distance and bowing to inexperienced inspectors. He is ready for some challenging undercover work for naval intelligence.

After drawing a cup of coffee, Rig picks up a copy of USA TODAY from the stack next to the coffee urn. He finds an overstuffed chair with an adjacent small table. He sets the coffee cup on the table, then flops his butt into the chair.

He glances over the uninteresting political stories on the front page. He turns the page and finds an interesting article on the second page.

UNIDENTIFIED ASSAULT FORCE SINKS BILLIONAIRE'S YACHT. During the dark hours of last Sunday morning, an assault force boarded the yacht owned by renowned international financier and movie producer Werner Braune and sank the yacht at anchor in Catalina Island's Avalon Bay. Braune was not onboard. The depth of the water resulted in the entire yacht being submerged.

After a complete search of the sunken yacht by divers, one body was found inside the yacht. The body of a passenger was found in the yacht's submerged security room. The body was identified as Mr. Owens by crewmen. Mr. Owens had a bullet hole in his chest. Coroner's report on Mr. Owens not yet complete.

Crewmembers also report that a woman passenger was onboard but is unaccounted for. None of the crew know the name of the woman passenger. Three crewmembers remain missing.

One crewman reports he encountered a member of the assault team who was well armed, dressed like a military commando, and wore a tactical hood. The crewman stated that the commando showed interest in the filing cabinets in the radio room. The crewman also stated that the commando led him off the yacht and into the water with a life vest before the yacht started to sink. The crewman said the commando wanted him to tell his story of the assault. Divers found the radio room filing cabinets open and empty.

Other crewmen report they were in the engine room when an outside explosion cracked the hull near the screw shafts and water poured into the engine room.

Werner Braune's whereabouts are unknown. Unsubstantiated reports claim Braune was airlifted off his hotel roof late Sunday afternoon.

Late last Sunday evening, authorities in Geneva Switzerland report that a hillside castle owned by a corporation of which Braune is the majority stock holder was attacked by rocket fire. No one was injured.

Investigations by California State Police and

Interpol are continuing.

Rig reads the article a second time. Then, he finishes the cup of coffee and returns to his office.

37

Movie Production Lot
Glendale, California

Terri Page sits in the production lot canteen and reads the second page article in *USA Today* about the sinking of Werner Braune's yacht. She worries about Werner Braune wreaking revenge on her someday. Denton's promise to keep Braune from taking any action does not fully comfort her.

When she reads about the body of Mr. Owens—Weston Pyth—being found, the image of her brother firing a bullet into Pyth's chest causes her heart to race.

She knows from the conversations onboard the *Frigg* that other *Paradisum* crew members were shot to death during her rescue. She asked Rig about those killings.

Rig responded, "I told those security men to drop their weapons and surrender. I told them they would not be harmed if they complied. But they opened fire on us instead. We had no choice but to shoot back."

Rig's explanation did not calm her, and Rig

saw that in her eyes.

Rig asked, "Terri, what do you think Pyth and Braune were going to do with you after they extorted Dad to do what they wanted?"

She had expressed horror at the implication.

"They would have killed you, Sis. They are evil sons-of-bitches."

Because of the terrifying situation that she experienced, she purchased a .38 caliber automatic and is attending a firing range course on how to use it. She also signed up for a self-defense course. The cost of the gun and courses gratefully paid by *The Guardians*.

Terri is still astonished and bewildered about the path Rig has taken. *My big brother is a government secret agent. Unbelievable!*

She has seen little of Rig since he joined the navy fifteen years ago. In the past when she thought about her brother, she held an image of a surfing teenager who had girls chasing him on the beach. Never again will she view him as that teenager.

38

Navy Radioman Schools
Naval Training Center San Diego

The school staff sits around a conference table and discusses the COMNAVEDTRA inspection report.

Commander Peterson tells Senior Chief Page, "I need a written objective to resolve these issues listed in the COMNAVEDTRA inspection report."

"I only see one item in the inspection report that affects my division," Rig responds. "The item that reports our lesson plans are riddled with grammar errors."

"That's the one," Commander Peterson confirms.

"I believe that discrepancy is invalid," Rig claims.

"Explain," Peterson orders in a slightly irritated tone.

"When the inspector first mentioned grammar errors, I asked him for examples. He showed me one of our lesson plans that he had marked up in red, displaying what he called errors. I advised the inspector that our lesson plans are written in outline, bullet format and that grammar does not apply. I showed him examples in the *Navy Instructor Manual*."

"What was his response?" the commander asks.

"He did not understand," Rig explains. "He never served in the navy and has never been an instructor. He is less than a year graduated from college with a bachelor's degree in education and a minor in English. He believes his opinion overrides the format specified in the *Navy Instructor Manual*. He does not understand the principle that when you claim a discrepancy you must cite the violated instruction or manual."

"The discrepancy is listed in the official inspection report," Commander Peterson emphasizes. "We must address it in our response."

"Okay," Rig responds. "I will write up justification for declaring it an invalid discrepancy, specifying that no reference for the discrepancy is cited."

"That's not what I mean," the commander states; irritation edging his tone. "I am not going to tell COMNAVEDTRA that their inspection report includes invalid discrepancies. I want you to write up an objective that says your division will review all lesson plans for compliance with the COMNAVEDTRA Instructors Manual with a deadline date of three months from now."

Several people at the table chuckle at the commander's clever solution.

When Rig finishes chuckling he says in an even-tempered tone, "Sounds like pandering, sir."

"Just three written sentences, Senior Chief. Then we can move on to more relevant issues."

Rig nods and expresses acceptance.

As the discussion moves on to issues not relevant to his responsibilities, Rig's mind reminisces those days past when he was involved in a more exciting undercover life in WESTPAC and Europe.

39

Task Force 152 Field Office
Naval Base San Diego

Jeff Borden asks Rig, "Have you been following the news about the sinking of Werner Braune's yacht in Catalina last month?"

"I remember hearing something about it on the news a couple of weeks ago. I did not pay much attention. Is it something important to ONI?"

"Do you know who Werner Braune is?" Borden asks.

"Only that his name is familiar, but I can't recall who he is."

"Braune is a Swiss citizen," Borden informs. "His parents were born in Germany but immigrated to England when they were twenty. Braune was born and raised in England. He is a rich man who owns multi-national businesses and is a well-known movie producer."

Rig nods acceptance of Braune's bio.

"Yesterday's *Washington Post* article revealed a lot of information not known before. Did you read it?"

Rig shakes his head, although he did read it three times.

"The yacht was sabotaged," Borden explains. "Explosives were detonated on the hull near the screws. The explosion cracked the hull. The engine room flooded. The crew jumped overboard.

"Only one crewman, the security room watch, encountered an intruder. The crewman described the intruder as an armed commando. The commando expressed interest in the radio room filing cabinets. The commando ordered the security watch to put on a life vest and then ordered the security watch to jump into the water before the explosion that sank the yacht. The commando wanted the security watch alive so he could later tell about his encounter with the commando. Those filing cabinets that the commando showed interest were found empty by divers.

"In the weeks following the yacht's sinking, the bodies of two crewman and one passenger have been discovered. All three of them were shot to death before the yacht sank. Two of them were security guards who roamed topside and their bodies washed ashore. The third, a passenger, was found in the security room of the sunken yacht.

"All crewmen have been accounted for. Only one person, a woman passenger, is missing. Crewmembers describe the woman as slim and attractive and say she was held captive in a locked cabin but was not found in the cabin when divers searched the sunken yacht. Divers reported the door to the woman's cabin was not locked.

"Attempts by Interpol to contact Werner Braune have failed. Braune's whereabouts are unknown, so says the article. The woman passenger remains unidentified.

"The body found in the security room of the sunken yacht was known as Mr. Owens to the crew. Under that name, the authorities could not trace his background. Then, the FBI and the newspapers received an anonymous call naming the dead Bill Owens as Weston Pyth, formerly of Long Beach, California and formerly employed by *The Long Beach Times*."

Rig fakes surprise and responds with sarcasm. "Well, finally, justice is served."

"Pyth disappeared several years ago," Borden explains. "Back then, authorities assumed he had been murdered by someone he pissed off in one of his newspaper articles. Instead, he was killed by a shot to the heart before the yacht was sunk.

"According to a file sent to me by headquarters, Pyth had claimed in his *Long Beach Times* articles that both you and your father were part of some conspiracy to destroy a labor union; that you and your father were going around blowing up union buildings and attacking union workers. Then, Pyth disappeared. Your father was questioned and his boat was searched."

Rig clarifies, "My father and I were cleared of charges and false accusations. That labor union threatened my family. They even sent hired killers after me. The FBI and Maryland State Police have all the evidence of the plot to kill me."

"Headquarters made that clear in their report," Borden informs.

"What does headquarters want from me?"

"The FBI also received from an anonymous source some files that linked Braune and Pyth in a conspiracy to sabotage Ronald Reagan's campaign. We believe those files came from aboard that yacht because some of the papers had the yachts letterhead. Since the media has not reported anything of what's in those files, we believe the anonymous source gave the papers only to the FBI, not the press."

Rig recalls Denton's plan for those radio room files. Copies of the files from Braune's yacht would go to the FBI; but only after the copies had been cleaned of any and all references to the Page family. Denton had also told Rig that copies of the files would be released to the press after additional information had been cleaned from the copies.

Borden continues, "The FBI distributed those files among the intelligence agencies. ONI already had a file on Braune. Several years ago, American agents began picking up bits of information that Braune was involved in sabotage against American companies that sell goods and services to the government.

"Currently, Braune's whereabouts are unknown. Both Interpol and the media are searching for him. He was last seen being helicoptered off the roof of his hotel in Catalina during the afternoon following the sinking of his yacht."

Borden picks up a thick file folder from his desk, "This is everything that ONI has on Pyth and Braune. Headquarters wants you to review the file and provide information you know about Pyth that is not in the file."

Borden hands Rig the file.

"How much time do I have?"

"A couple of days. That file must remain here in the office."

"Okay. I will spend some time on it now and finish it tomorrow."

Before he opens the file, Rig has already decided not to add anything. He knows that if he adds information, he will be questioned on where he gained the information.

40

Venice, California

Cassandra Reynolds watches the nightly TV news in the two-room apartment that she shares with another aging, semi-retired actress. When she sees the two side-by-side photographs of Mr. Owens and Mr. Pyth. She cries, knowing that the money promised her will never come.

When she called the lawyer yesterday morning, she was informed that the project to put her on national TV with the claim she had been raped by Ronald Reagan was terminated. When she asked why, the lawyer said, "Funding for the project has been discontinued."

She stares at the stack of utility and grocery bills on the coffee table and worries how she will pay them.

Then, a thought comes to her. She knows several rich movie executives who have been critical of Ronald Reagan; something about Reagan's actions when he was governor of California. She decides to peddle her story to them. Omitting, of course, that her accusation of rape is false.

41

Apennine Mountains
Northeast of Rome, Italy

When a majority of *The Trajan Consortium* directors want an emergency director's meeting, that majority selects a scheduling committee. When the dates and place of the meeting are settled, the *demand to attend* is sent to all directors. By their own rules, all directors are required to attend emergency directors' meetings.

During the existence of *The Trajan Consortium*, this is the third time an emergency directors meeting has been demanded and scheduled. The first was 1971 when President Richard Nixon ended the United States gold standard. The second time was 1973 when the Organization of Arab Petroleum Exporting Countries proclaimed an oil embargo against countries supporting Israel.

This third emergency meeting is being held at an Italian mountaintop retreat owned by one of the directors. The only transportation to the mountaintop retreat is by helicopter or by aerial cable car. During the three days that the directors occupy the retreat, the aerial cable car system is shutdown.

On the second day of their stay at the retreat, The directors of *The Trajan Consortium* hold their emergency meeting to discuss Werner Braune and the America situation.

Because Braune's actions are under scrutiny, the vice-chairman conducts the meeting and the questioning.

"The American newspapers are reporting more than what I know about what happened aboard the *Paradisum*," Braune tells the directors.

"What can you tell us that the American newspapers do not know?" asks the vice-chairman.

"The missing woman passenger, I know who she is."

"She is alive?" asks a director.

"Yes. One of my American operatives reports she lives a normal life with no indications that her life was interrupted for a few days."

"Has she not reported what happened to the authorities?"

"Appears not," Braune responds.

Several directors shake their heads. "Does not make sense," comments one of the directors. Several others nod and express agreement.

"Yes, it is a mystery," Braune agrees. "Just as mysterious as who attacked my organization and sank my yacht and bombed *Le Haut* Château."

One of the directors suggest, "Could be a competitor behind all this and they paid her to be quiet."

Braune adds, "All of you have read the death threat note they sent me. If I violate their conditions, I will be killed. We should consider that some of those conditions are of no concern to them and are just diversions to confuse us— to keep us guessing as to who they are and their ultimate objective."

The vice-chairman says, "We need a complete dossier on this woman and her family."

"A dossier has been completed," Braune informs. "I will distribute copies to all of you."

"What files did they take from the yacht?" asks the vice-chairman.

"All of the communications files and codes and all of Mr. Owens's files. Owens's files contained details and financial records of all his operations to destroy Ronald Reagan."

Everyone gasps at that revelation.

The vice-chairman speaks for everyone in the room when he says, "That is extremely disturbing. We are vulnerable not knowing who holds those files."

Braune recommends, "I propose that we commit resources to uncover the organization that sank the *Paradisum* and destroy them."

"I second that proposal," another director declares.

"Those in favor raise your hand," the vice-chairman directs.

All in the room raise their hands.

42

Sacramento California

Mark Ringard calls his old army buddy, longtime friend and sometimes election fraud coconspirator, Bob Latori.

After several rings, Bob answers. "California Election Commission, Bob Latori."

"Hi, Bob. Mark Ringard."

"Hi, Mark. I've been expecting your call."

Ringard says, "I am assuming that Mr. Owens's request has been overcome by events."

"Yes," Latori affirms, "but others are interested. I will arrange another meeting.

"Aren't you worried about Owens's missing files?" Ringard asked in a concerned tone.

"What missing files?"

"It was in the news reports," Ringard specifies. "Files are missing from the room next to where Owens was found. Our names could be in those files."

"Oh, shit!" Latori blurts. "I did not connect

those dots."

"What are we going to do?" Ringard asks anxiously.

"We should not honor any more requests. Let's just do our jobs."

"I like that plan," Ringard says with a sigh of relief.

43

Phoenix, Arizona

Cameron Luce sits at his desk in the ACP Development Department. He stares at the two pictures of Weston Pyth in *The Washington Post*. One picture shows Pyth with long hair and scraggily beard when he worked for *The Long Beach Times*. The other picture shows the clean-cut, conservative-looking 'Bill Owens' from a fake-passport picture.

The deadline for Luce to deliver the modified code came and went, and no one contacted him. Luce concludes that the organization Owens represented has been destroyed— probably funded by Werner Braune. The newspaper article reports that Werner Braune has not been seen or heard from since being helicoptered off the roof of his hotel on Catalina Island.

Luce used his computer and research skills in an attempt to uncover the owners of ACP. After a week of searching, he tracked ownership to a Swiss company owned by a holding company. He encountered a brick wall when he attemptod to uncover the names of those who owned the holding company. Luce concludes that Braune must be the owner or co-owner of that holding company because only a rich and powerful man like Braune could establish such a brick wall.

He pulls the terminal keyboard toward him, logs into the mainframe computer located in the next room, brings up the altered vote counting code, and deletes it.

Luce worries about the missing files mentioned in the news reports. He fears that the FBI may come knocking on his door.

44

Reno, Nevada

Randy Gough chuckles as he reads the newspaper article that exposes a partnership between Weston Pyth and the international billionaire Werner Braune. The article speculates as to what Pyth, a Marxist, and Braune, a European billionaire had in common. The article reports that Braune has often been categorized as anti-American with fascist principles.

The partnership between Pyth and Braune does not surprise Gough. Representatives of such partnerships have contacted Gough many times. Their objective was always the same. Rich foreign capitalists looking for dirt on presidential candidates or on cabinet nominees whose foreign policies would negatively affect the capitalist's international businesses. However, a *commando* raid and three murders against such partnerships is something new.

During the early years, he provided dirt for the communist cause and did not request payment. Because he offered dirt for free, he was bombarded with requests that kept him so busy that his earnings from his day-jobs suffered. Attempting to live like a communist in a capitalist society was difficult and costly.

He began charging a fee for his dirt services. At first, he agreed to payment after the dirt was nationally published. But after so many projects were not published he demanded money up front, as he did with Owens—Pyth.

He chuckles again as he remembers all those fresh, eager communist faces who rise every decade claiming they have a successful formula for an American collectivist society.

Gough is not concerned about his name being in Owens' missing files. There is nothing illegal in the business conducted between Gough and Pyth. If Gough's name is publicly mentioned as an associate of Pyth's, such notoriety will bring him more business.

"Not my first rodeo," he says to himself.

45

Task Force 152 Field Office
Naval Base San Diego

"You can stop tailing Cleo," Borden informs. "Her real name is Patricia Cleo Harmon. She is a navy brat and an ex-navy wife who has several restraining orders issued against her ex-husband. Her ex is currently stationed on a ship homeported in Pearl.

"She is not using an alias as we first thought. Instead of renting her own apartment, she rents a room in other people's homes or apartments. She pays cash for everything. Her car is registered in Texas with her parents address on her driver's license. She is employed by one of those national temp agencies that rents people out to businesses. The agency safeguards her personal information. She does all that to make it harder for her ex to find her."

"I am glad to hear that," Rig says while expressing amusement. "She sounds like a smart lady."

"Are you ready for another assignment," Borden asks.

"Sure."

Borden hands Rig a photograph.

Rig studies the color photograph of a tall and thin First Class Electronics Technician wearing summer whites. Five ribbons and a submarine warfare pin are displayed above his left breast pocket. The sailor's pitch-black mustache and hair contrast against his pale white skin.

"That's an official awards photo," Borden informs. "ET1 Jansen was selected Command Sailor of the Quarter earlier this year."

"What command?" Rig asks while looking at the photo. "He looks familiar."

"He's assigned to the submarine tender at Point Loma submarine base, Repair Department. He's a SINS tech."

Rig turns his eyes toward Borden and asks, "What's his story?"

"He's a homosexual. We believe he has been compromised by Soviet agents and is being blackmailed. Jansen provides classified information to his Soviet contact, and his Soviet contact does not expose Jansen's homosexual activities to the navy. We believe Jansen is being forced to recruit other homosexual sailors into a spy ring controlled by the

Soviets."

"Such a sad situation," Rig comments. "If homosexuals were allowed to serve openly, they would not be targets for foreign espionage."

"That's true," Borden agrees, "maybe someday. Would certainly lighten our workload."

"Would lighten a lot of workloads," Rig adds.

"That's for sure," Borden agrees.

"So, what's my task with Jansen?" Rig inquires.

"We need you to follow him, take pictures of everyone he associates with off base, collect their license plate numbers, their addresses, their names.

"Like before, all your off-base surveillance must be in full disguise. There must be nothing on you or in your cover car that can be traced to your real identity."

Rig says confidently, "Yes . . . disguise . . . I get it. This is not my first time out in the cold."

"Your mission is easy. We have already attached a radio beacon to the underside of his car, and there is a beacon tracker installed in your cover car. All you need to do is track, record, and report."

Rig sighs deeply and stares into space. Again, he reminiscences those days-past of a more adventurous undercover life in WESTPAC and Europe.

46

Soviet Consulate
San Francisco, California

The office of the KGB Supervisor is second in size only to the consul general's office but is first in amenities. The décor is traditional Russian, including a small bar stocked with quality Russian Vodka and the finest American bourbon. A portrait of Alexei Kosygin hangs on the wall behind the supervisor's desk.

Jack sits in a chair across the desk from the KGB Supervisor. They discuss the impact of Weston Pyth's death on their espionage operations.

Jack briefs his supervisor. "Pyth's death does not have a significant effect on our operations to sabotage the Reagan campaign. We have plenty of operatives working on that. And the Americans have their own political parties and press conducting their own misinformation campaigns.

"My focus is finding a replacement operative to infiltrate Werner Braune's top circle of advisors. Braune is our possible path into *The*

Trajan Consortium."

The KGB Supervisor informs, "Central reports that Braune is moving his North American headquarters to Europe. Intelligence sources reveal that Braune is under a death sentence should he ever return to America."

"For Central to know that," Jack responds, "we must already have someone inside *The Trajan Consortium* at a high level, probably in Europe."

"My judgement also," Jack's supervisor submits. "Central directed that *The Trajan Consortium* is no longer among our priorities. Central ordered that we discover who sank Werner Braune's yacht and forced him out of America. Any organization that powerful and well-funded is a threat to our operations. I am assigning you the task of discovering who they are."

Jack asks, "Did Central provide any intel along with that directive?"

"Yes. The files taken from the yacht during the commando raid are being passed to the American FBI."

"Hmm," Jack responds, "that means they are not a lawless organization. Do we have copies?"

"Not yet," the KGB Supervisor responds. "The Washington office is working on that."

"In one of Pyth's intel dumps to me, he provided a list of the yacht's crew with their backgrounds. I will start with them."

The KGB supervisor grins and asks, "So all these years, Pyth never suspected he was working for the Soviet Union and not that Weathermen organization?"

"Correct?" Jack responds proudly.

"And all the others you control, they too believe they are serving the Weathermen?"

"The Weathermen or other American underground communist organizations," Jack answers in a confident tone.

"Excellent!" the KGB supervisor responds enthusiastically. "Continue to brief me weekly. I will write the reports to Central."

47

The Page Residence
Seal Beach, California

Rig, his two sisters, and his parents sit down to Sunday dinner. As they pass the plates of food around the table, the conversation turns to news of Weston Pyth's death.

James Page says, "I would give up a year's earnings to know what Pyth and Braune were plotting. I bet it was something big, corrupt, and political."

Margaret Page, Rig's mother, looks at Terri and asks, "What's the gossip in the movie industry?"

"Werner Braune has two movies in pre-production," Terry informs. "None of the contracts have reached their lock-in date, and people are worried about the productions being cancelled."

Kate Page, Rig's other sister, adds, "I would like to know more about who attacked them and sank Braune's yacht. The papers say a commando raid but did not specify military or terrorist. No one has claimed responsibility and only one *commando* was encountered by crewmembers."

"Why must it be a terrorist organization if it's not military?" Rig challenges.

"Who else could it be?" Kate questions sincerely.

"There are secret organizations that *fight for truth, justice, and the American way,*" Rig asserts.

Kate asks, "How do we know that some so-called secret organization killed three people and sank Braune's yacht for *truth, justice, and the American way?*"

Terri Page stares at her brother and wonders how he will answer that question."

Rig explains, "Pyth was an underground Marxist activist who staged violent events where people were brutally hurt and killed, and who was funded by an anti-American international billionaire. America is a better place with Pyth dead and with Werner Braune hiding in Europe."

"How do you know what Pyth was doing?" Margaret Page asks.

"As a naval communicator, I have access to mountains of classified information. Some of Pyth's actions will be made public on Monday.

So, until the information is released, I ask you to keep it to yourselves."

"It doesn't make sense," James Page declares. "Commies like Pyth committing evil and violent acts in collusion with rich foreign capitalists. That's scary and makes me wonder how often that happens."

"The end justifies the means," Rig states.

"The end justifies the means," Terri repeats curiously. "That sounds dark. Does it mean what I think it means?"

"It's a slogan used by Marxists to justify their evil actions," Rig explains. "It means that achieving world socialism is so essential to social justice that any evil act to achieve it is justified."

"Hopefully, they will never come to America," Margaret Page says; her tone filled with angst.

"They're already here, Mom," Rig declares in a tone of warning. "Not foreigners but American socialists and American communists—the enemy within. They are infiltrating every level of American society—the education system, judicial system, the media, and government. Unless average Americans wake up to the coming danger, voters will be electing socialists and communists as mayors, legislators, governors, and president. Constitutional liberties and The American Dream will be dead."

The Page family sits in silence as they ponder the possibility of Americans not waking up and Rig's prediction becoming reality.

* * * * *

"Freedom is never more than one generation away from extinction. We didn't pass it to our children in the bloodstream. It must be fought for, protected, and handed on for them to do the same, or one day we will spend our sunset years telling our children and our children's children what it was once like in the United States where men were free."

— **Ronald Reagan**

* * * * *

"The inherent vice of capitalism is the unequal sharing of blessings; the inherent virtue of socialism is the equal sharing of miseries."
— **Winston Churchill**

Made in the USA
Las Vegas, NV
14 February 2021

17856894R00154